LET SLEEPING GHOSTS LIE

A REAPER WITCH MYSTERY

ELLE ADAMS

To be notified when Elle Adams's next book is released, sign up to her author newsletter.

Carey and I walked towards the abandoned house as the sun sank in the darkening sky. Her bright yellow goggles bounced on her forehead as we walked, while Casper, her familiar, walked at her side. The little black cat was scared of ghosts, but I'd convinced her to bring him along today in the hopes that he'd be able to conquer his fear.

I had to admit I was having second thoughts. The poor cat jumped every time my brother, Mart, went close to him. As far as ghosts went, Mart was pretty much harmless, but Casper was the jumpiest cat I'd ever encountered, while Mart's tendency to take things too far didn't help. As I had no familiar of my own, my brother was the closest I'd get to one. If anything, he was more high maintenance than most familiars were, and annoying in the way only a sibling could be.

"Here we are," said Carey. "This is Healey House."

The old brick house sat in a sunken area at the side of the river, nestled in a swampy garden overgrown with weeds. It was one of many houses which had been abandoned following the floods in town twenty-odd years ago, and rumour had it that some ghostly activity had picked up inside the house in the last week or two. Carey and I kept our ears open for any gossip and we'd failed to unearth anything on our last ghost-hunting mission, but I hoped this one would end in success for both of us.

No obvious spiritual activity pinged on my radar, however, aside from the usual transparent figures floating in the background as we walked. As an ex-Reaper, moving to a town as haunted as Hawkwood Hollow had been an adjustment and a half. The town's everyday ghosts who wandered the streets mostly left me alone now, to my relief, but that didn't change the fact that I was a magnet for spirits. In other words, the perfect work partner for a teenage ghost blogger. Which was just one reason I'd agreed to accompany Carey to Healey House in the hopes that she'd get some good footage of this elusive spirit.

Carey sprang up to the doorstep and pushed the door inwards with a creak. The hallway smelled of mould and neglect, shadows spilling across bare floorboards patched with rotting scraps of carpet. We both wore dark clothing —my idea—though I could see Carey's signature bright socks poking out from under the hems of her jeans.

Carey pulled the ghost goggles over her eyes, and there was a click as she turned on the microphone. "Here we are, in Healey House, abandoned after the floods in the town of Hawkwood Hollow two decades ago. I'm with Maura, the Reaper Witch, as we attempt to unearth the secrets of the—"

She cut off in a yelp as she tripped over something in the hall, catching her balance on the nearest door frame.

"You okay?" I asked, ignoring Mart's laughter in the background.

"Yep," she said. "I think there's a loose floorboard somewhere underneath there."

"Old houses can be hazardous," I said. "Careful. We don't want any of us getting injured."

I trod across the bare floorboards, which were covered in a thick layer of damp and creaked with each step. The floor seemed sturdy enough, though, so I didn't see the need to employ my trusty Reaper's shadows to catch my balance.

Carey's familiar didn't seem to agree. Casper set one paw into the hall, hissed, and recoiled back into the doorway.

"It's okay, Casper," Carey called. "It's safe."

I beckoned to her familiar. "I think he's more bothered by the wet floor than the ghosts."

"Boo," Mart said from behind him.

The little cat yelped and backed up into the doorway, his ears pricked.

"Mart!" I said. "Cut that out."

"Spoilsport." He floated into the hall, arms spread wide as though he could still touch the walls, as I led the way through into an equally damp living room.

"Any ghosts yet?" Carey held her ghost goggles at the ready. Homemade and fitted with lenses which could see ghosts but not much else, the goggles were bright red in colour and stood out against the dark backdrop of the house. The microphone was a neat addition, but she had yet to perfect it so that it picked up on ghosts as well as living people's voices.

"Not that I can see." I strained my ears, but I heard

3

ELLE ADAMS

nothing upstairs. "Or hear. I'd keep the goggles off until we're close."

"Will do."

In the lead, I waded through the living room, wishing I'd worn more suitable shoes. My feet squelched along the soggy carpet and sank into dampness, while Carey spoke into the microphone.

"Citizens of Hawkwood Hollow have heard screaming from this house on and off for years," she said. "However, in the last few weeks, the reports of ghostly activity have picked up. Will we be the first to catch a glimpse of the infamous spirit?"

"The only thing you'll catch in here is a cold," Mart said.

I withdrew my foot from a particularly damp patch of carpet and spotted a few lines of text scrawled on the wall in thick marker. I moved closer, trying to read them, but the lines appeared to be made up of symbols which weren't in any language I could read. They looked vaguely like the sort of runes one might use in a spell, but I wasn't exactly up to speed on my knowledge of the latest arcane symbols. "I think someone was casting a spell in here."

"Ooh." Carey bounded up behind me. "There's an old rumour that this house was once used as a meeting place for a cult."

"That, or it's just graffiti," said Mart. "The house was abandoned twenty years ago, not two hundred. It's hardly an ancient ruin."

"Mart, your optimism is infectious," I told him. "Let's see if we can find anything else."

Carey, who took my brother's interruptions in stride —perhaps surprisingly considering she couldn't actually

4

see or hear him—backed into the hallway and headed for the stairs.

I extricated my feet from the swampy floor and turned away from the wall, when a sudden jolt of coldness shot through me like ice water flowing through my veins. My head snapped up, my skin chilled, and shadows crept around my feet.

What the—?

"Maura?" said Carey. "Did you see something?"

She couldn't see the shadows—the house was too dark—but she'd probably felt the temperature drop and seen my change in expression. But it wasn't a ghost I'd sensed. My Reaper powers had kicked in for a different reason.

Someone, somewhere in town, had died.

"No, I don't see anything." Even though I was telling the truth, it felt like a lie. "Mart, any ghosts?"

"Do I not count?" He pouted.

So he hadn't sensed the chill of someone passing from the living world into the afterlife. He'd left most of his own Reaper powers behind when he'd died, so it wasn't entirely a surprise, but the knowledge that I alone had sensed it made me want to leave the house altogether. I tried to calm my breathing, reasoning that it didn't necessarily mean a bad omen for our ghost-hunting mission. Back when I'd first started my Reaper training, I'd grown used to the sudden bursts of cold whenever someone in the general area passed on, but my abilities had gone into hibernation for years after I'd turned my back on the position and left my home. I couldn't say I knew why they'd chosen this moment to switch back on, but it wasn't worth ditching the ghost hunt for. Not if it was just a regular death which I wasn't supposed to be aware of anyway.

Besides, dealing with the dead was the job for the local Reaper, and I wasn't one. Since old Harold had retired years ago, the only thing he did with his scythe was hang his coat on it, but that didn't mean he wouldn't have stern words for me if I reaped a soul without his knowledge. I'd rather not get into another spat with him, so I did my best to put all thoughts of Reaper business to the back of my mind and continued searching the house.

No spiritual disturbances presented themselves. Not so much as a slamming door or a faint breeze which indicated a ghostly presence. Except for Mart, of course, who offered a running commentary which made me glad Carey's microphone couldn't pick up on the sound of ghosts speaking. Despite all our efforts, though, the spirits we actually wanted to find didn't materialise. Maybe the new death, whoever it was, had scared them off.

When I was alone in the hall waiting for Carey to finish searching the living room again, Mart floated up to me. "Who walked on your grave?"

"Mart, someone died." I spoke in a low voice. "My Reaper powers kicked in and told me someone passed on. No mistaking it."

His brow wrinkled. "Seriously? You sure it wasn't just this creepy old house?"

"You told me you didn't see any other ghosts in here, either," I pointed out. "Anyway, the feeling is different when a ghost appears. You should know."

"I haven't been able to use my Reaper powers since before I died," he said. "You don't have to rub it in."

"I'm not. I'm just trying to figure out what happened

here." I tried to put on a neutral expression when Carey emerged from the living room. "Can you have a look outside?"

"Well, all *right.*" Mart floated away through the front door, his transparent form vanishing through the wooden surface.

Carey halted in front of me. "What's up?"

"My brother's being his usual helpful self." I spotted poor Casper shivering in the shadows, his fur standing on end. Sometimes I wondered if the cat was more in tune with all things ghostly than most witches, but even familiars weren't able to sense death the way Reapers could. "Not sure we're going to find anything in here, to tell you the truth."

"Me neither," she said. "We can always come back another night. I'm sure the ghost will show up eventually, if we're persistent enough."

"You never know," I said. "Look how long it took us to lure out Mrs Renner, and that ended up being worth it."

If you discounted the part where Mrs Renner's old house had nearly collapsed on top of us, that is. We were lucky we'd got any footage out of that mess, but Carey's account of the events of a few weeks ago on her blog had proven a big hit, and she now had subscribers in the double figures. While I'd once vowed never to use my ghost-hunting abilities publicly again, it was nice to have something to focus on aside from my life's long streak of bad decisions and the knowledge that I was thoroughly disappointing both my Reaper father and my witch mother.

In fairness, I had a steady job now for the first time in a long while. Over the last few weeks, I'd been working part-time at the inn which Carey's family owned, and as a bonus, I got all my meals for free and a roof over my head. The least I could do was give Carey a helping hand with her ghost blog, since that was the reason I'd ended up coming to Hawkwood Hollow to begin with.

With Casper padding along at our side, Carey and I left the house and closed the wooden door behind us.

Mart floated over to us, barely visible in the gloom. "Hey, there's trouble up on the bridge over there. Maybe that's our dead body."

Uh-oh. Motioning Carey to stay back, I peered up at the bridge, where a group of people gathered—including Detective Drew Gardener, chief of police here in Hawkwood Hollow. Tall and broad-shouldered with longish dark hair, he cut a striking figure amongst the crowd even from a distance. My heart flipped a little when he caught my eye, talking to someone on the bridge.

"Did something happen?" Carey said. "That's Hayley over there, from the inn."

She quickened her pace, as did I, and we walked up the sloping road to the bridge and reached the gathering crowd. Aside from the police, who were mostly shifters, a few witches and wizards had wandered onto the bridge from the inn. Hayley, my main co-worker aside from Carey and her mother, stood among them, her expression anxious and her spiky blond hair ruffled from the cold wind.

When I saw the body lying on the old stone bridge, my heart sank. I didn't recognise her, but the woman lay still, her hair plastered to her face by river water and weeds clinging to her clothes. My Reaper instincts had been closer to home than I'd realised.

"I just levitated her out the river," said a wizard wearing a red hat, his voice slurring. "We were on our way back from the bar when Archie nearly fell off the bridge. I levitated him to safety, and then I saw her floating in the water."

"That's Harriet Langley," said someone else. "I know her. She's a witch, and she works at the hospital."

"What was she doing out alone?" said another witch.

"Going to the bar at the Riverside Inn, I'd wager."

"Or going home."

Carey hovered on the balls of her feet. "Should we find out what happened?"

"We have to walk across the bridge to get home anyway," I reminded her in an undertone. "C'mon, let's head back to the inn. I'll talk to the detective on the way."

The two of us walked onto the bridge, and Drew gave me a nod when he saw me approaching.

I halted in front of him. "Hey."

"Maura," he said. "And Carey. What're you doing out this late?"

"Ghost hunting," I said. "What's going on?"

"I'm afraid someone drowned in the river," he said. "I'm still trying to piece together what happened. Did you see anyone when you left the inn?"

I shook my head. "Nah, we went straight to Healey House, down there on the other side of the bridge. Didn't see anyone on the way." Living or dead. Not that most people would make that distinction. I alone saw the half-dozen pale transparent figures drifting around—but none of them resembled the woman lying on the bridge. Her own ghost wouldn't appear until later, if at all.

"Are you taking Carey back to the inn?" he asked.

"Sure." I nudged Carey in the arm. "You okay?"

Carey had gone pale, clutching Casper in her arms, but she gave a mute nod.

"I'll see you later," I added to the detective. "Better get home."

There was nothing I could do for the victim now. My Reaper senses hadn't told me to escort her soul into the afterlife and I couldn't see or sense her ghost at all. Not surprising, given that the town was swimming in so many spirits that I'd never get a moment's peace if my Reaper senses reacted to every one of them. There was usually a gap between when someone died and when their ghost returned, besides.

Carey and I crossed the bridge and reached the cobbled street on the other side, near the Riverside Inn. The inn, owned by Carey's family, also included a restaurant and bar which were popular with the town's residents, and the lights inside the bar looked warm and inviting in the cold night.

"Poor guy," I said. "I get the feeling Drew was supposed to have the night off and didn't expect a bunch of drunk wizards to find a body in the river."

Come to think of it, my Reaper senses had reacted less than half an hour ago. Had the witch really been out alone when she'd drowned? Given how quickly the crowd had appeared, I couldn't say for certain, but if I'd gone to look outside when my senses had reacted, I might've seen more.

There wasn't anything I could have done. It wasn't like I knew it was coming, did I?

Carey put down Casper to walk at her side. "Do you think her ghost might show up?"

"Maybe." I slowed my pace as we neared the inn. "I should probably talk to the detective tomorrow."

"Why?" asked Carey.

I hesitated. "Because… because my Reaper senses went off. When we were in the house. They told me someone died."

Her eyes rounded. "Really? Did you know it was her?"

"No," I said. "My Reaper senses aren't that specific. All that happens is that it suddenly goes cold, but I can't tell who died until I see the body. I didn't even know she was that close to Healey House."

Her brow furrowed. "So what are you going to tell the detective?"

"I don't know," I said. "This is the police's job, not mine. I have no idea why my Reaper senses reacted the way they did. They haven't for years."

With one exception: the time they'd reacted to Mrs Renner's ghost the week I'd first come to town. I'd been fighting to save Carey's life at the time, and I didn't need a sixth sense to tell me a powerful ghost was on the horizon. The sense that reacted when someone died, though… that one had been dormant for much longer. If I'd been an active Reaper, the same sense would have dragged me to the body in order for me to escort the soul into the afterlife. With the scythe I didn't have, because I hadn't been an active Reaper for years. What had my senses expected me to do, really?

"Why not?" she asked.

"Because I quit using my Reaping skills," I said. "Except in extreme circumstances."

"Like the other week," she said.

"Yeah." I'd begun to regret bringing up the subject at

all. This wasn't my responsibility. I'd begun to settle into Hawkwood Hollow, ghosts and all, but that didn't mean I wanted to be its Reaper. That road only led to trouble. Reapers stood on the edge of paranormal society, as a rule, and for most of them, nothing mattered more than their job. They didn't have friends or families. They certainly didn't go sneaking around old houses in the hope of getting decent footage of local ghosts for a teenager's blog.

Even the local Reaper didn't act like a typical one, come to that. Since he'd retired without an apprentice, nobody else in town was inclined to take his place. I'd spent my first couple of weeks in town on tenterhooks, expecting an ambassador from the Reaper Council to show up at any minute and send in someone to take on the role instead, but I'd got complacent. Maybe I shouldn't have done. I mean, the place was swarming with ghosts. Someone aside from me was bound to notice the town had slipped through the cracks eventually, and I didn't look forward to that day with any level of pleasure.

I'd never been good at settling down. The last few weeks in Hawkwood Hollow had been among the most settled I'd ever felt during my time living in the magical world, and the notion of my Reaper powers getting in the way wasn't a pleasant one. At the very least, an inconvenient awareness whenever anyone passed away would dampen my attempts to blend in, to say the least.

Yet this situation might be a one-off. I hoped it was, anyway. For now, Carey and I walked towards the welcoming warmth of the Riverside Inn.

2

Carey and I entered the inn's lobby, which connected to the restaurant via a set of glass doors. A few patrons occupied the bar, mostly witches and wizards, but given the number of abandoned tables with half-empty glasses sitting on them, I assumed the majority of them had gone to see what was going on over at the bridge.

Carey's mother, Allie, waved at us from across the room. She shared her daughter's curly dark hair, though hers was streaked with grey, and I suspected that if I looked under the hem of her deep green cloak, I'd see the same bright red socks that Carey wore. "What's going on out there?"

"Someone died," I said. "Drowned in the river."

Her face fell. "Oh, no. Who?"

"Harriet Langley," Carey said. "The detective was there on the bridge, talking to the people who found her."

"A group of drunk wizards on their way home from

the bar," I added. "Hayley was there, too. I guess everyone went to check it out."

"Oh, she must have been on her way home from her shift," said Allie. "I wondered where everyone went, but I have to keep an eye on things in here now the local wizards have picked out this place as their meeting point."

"Was she in here, too?" I asked. "Harriet, I mean."

"No, she wasn't," said Allie. "Not today, anyway. I didn't know her well, but she was a coven member as well as a nurse at the local hospital. I feel sorry for her family. I do hope the police can get answers."

"Me too." After Carey's relentless questioning, the last thing I needed was to face another round from her mother, so I opted not to bring up my Reaper senses' ill-timed warning. I'd assumed that part of my life was long behind me, and while I made use of my skills to help Carey hunt for ghosts, that wasn't the same as embracing the half of me which always ended up getting me into trouble.

In a way, I'd always stand apart from others, what with being half Reaper and half witch. Didn't mean I needed to encourage my outsider status, though. Being treated like a pariah got old fast. I hadn't known Harriet, besides. I was better off leaving this one in the police's hands. Or so I told myself.

I headed for the stairs up to the first floor, and the inn's room which had become my new home. Despite my best efforts, though, the old sense of guilt and responsibility knocked on the back of my skull like my father's disapproving voice muttering in my ear.

"Bloody Reaper skills," I muttered. "You can't switch

on and off whenever you feel like it. That's not how it's supposed to work."

Like it or not, though, if the switch had flipped, it might well be permanent. Which meant unless I found a way to turn it off, I'd get an alert every time someone died, no matter who or where. Talk about the worst alarm clock ever.

Mart flew past me down the carpeted corridor of the inn. "I don't know why you're complaining. I remember you were upset when your Reaper skills first switched off."

"That's because I thought I needed them to hunt ghosts," I told him. "I know better now. Anyway, not everyone turns into a ghost when they die."

"Here, there's a good chance of it," he said.

He had a point. There were more ghosts than living people here in Hawkwood Hollow, and I'd banished a grand total of two of them since my arrival. By now, I was getting used to seeing groups of spirits around and they mostly left me alone. But the more I embraced my Reaper side, the more attention I'd draw from both sides of the grave. Which really wasn't ideal.

"Maybe, but that doesn't mean I need to start keeping tabs on them." I dug in my pocket and pulled out the key to my room, which was down the corridor from the suite Carey shared with her mother. It was a nice room, one of the many perks of working here at the inn, and it came with zero ghosts, except the one who followed me everywhere I went. No complaints from me.

I unlocked the door and entered my room. Set out like a typical hotel room with a double bed and pale wooden furniture, it was neat and fairly bare. I kept one suitcase of clothes, along with my broomstick and some other essentials, and that was all I needed. I was more than ready to flop onto the bed and sleep, but there was one slight issue.

There was already a ghost in the room, and it wasn't my brother. She was a young woman, maybe in her twenties, with expressive dark eyes and a mournful expression on her face. Her faded cloak spread across my bed as she sprawled out as though the room belonged to her.

"Hey," I said. "Um, who are you?"

She leapt to her feet. "You can see me?"

"Yes…" I closed the door behind me. "I don't mean to be rude, but this room's taken."

"By both of us," added Mart.

She looked between the two of us, her brow furrowing. "Are you sure?"

"Yes, I'm sure," I said. "I work here at the inn, and I'm staying in this room. I'm Maura, and this is Mart, my brother. Who are you?"

"Mandy," she said. "Sorry, but I have to stay here."

"Why?" Past experience had taught me the hard way that ticking off the ghost would only make things harder for all of us, so I'd prefer to tread carefully if possible. I still didn't know how much power she possessed, after all. Usually there was no way to tell from outside appearances if a ghost could hardly lift a piece of paper—or if they could knock out the electricity in the whole building. Unless I wanted everyone else in the inn to find out about my new visitor, I'd better not risk it.

"It's safe in here," she said.

"There are a dozen or more empty rooms on this floor alone," I pointed out. "I'm a light sleeper, and Mart likes his space. If you want to ask for an empty room, I can speak to Allie."

She shook her head. "I don't want to be a bother. I'll just… stay here. In this corner."

Mart scoffed. "You most certainly will not. How long have you been a ghost, anyway? I got here first."

"I don't know." She floated into the corner and hovered warily on the spot as though she was afraid that Mart would chase her off if she got too close to him. "I don't know."

"Just bloody wonderful, that," said Mart. "How'd you die?"

"I don't *know.*" She burst into loud, gulping sobs, and sank into a sitting position in the corner of the room.

"Wait." I approached her, and she flinched away from me. "Ignore my brother. I'm not going to hurt you."

"Don't ignore me," said Mart. "Everyone knows I'm really in charge here. Anyway, if you're going to let her camp out in here, then it's worth finding out how she died. I'm not the one who'll be in trouble if an axe murderer shows up at the door."

"Mart, quiet." I turned back to the ghost. "How long have you been dead?"

"A while," she said between sobs. "I don't… remember."

Oh, boy. It wasn't unheard of for ghosts who'd stuck around for a long time to forget how long they'd been dead, but a hysterical ghost was not what I needed to deal with at the moment.

Thanks for that, Mart.

———

After a sleepless night, it was something of a relief to go downstairs to the restaurant to find the place heaving with gossip about the body found in the river the previous evening. Compared to the hours I'd spent calming the ghost and listening to Mart bemoan her presence in my room, I'd gladly take the distraction. When my brother's loud singing hadn't convinced the newcomer to leave, he'd resorted to levitating things around and turning the lights on and off, until I'd yelled at him and caused the guests in the room above mine to hammer on the floor in annoyance.

And to think I'd assumed my reawakening Reaper senses would be the most irritating event of the night.

I picked up a plate and took it to the buffet tables at the back of the restaurant, loading it with breakfast before joining Carey and Casper at a nearby table. Carey had her ghost goggles plugged into my old laptop with the video of our visit to Healey House playing out on the screen, and she smiled as I sat down opposite her.

"I can't get anything good out of this footage," she said. "Maybe next time you can ask Mart to levitate something."

I yawned. "He won't do something like that without payment."

Her brow wrinkled. "How do you pay a ghost?"

"Usually in hot showers," I said. "He claims he can feel the warmth of the water. Don't ask me how."

"Wow," she said. "Guess I don't know as much about ghosts as I thought I did."

"Believe it or not, I don't know everything about ghosts," I said. "All of them are different, which typically depends on what they were like when they were alive. Mart is a special case, anyway."

For several reasons. One was that he'd been a Reaper himself when he was alive. Another was that in the process of using my magic to bind him to me, I'd made him stronger than a regular ghost. While I sometimes wondered if he'd always want that, he'd already had a chance to leave and had chosen to stay, for what it was worth.

Mandy, on the other hand, was going to be a problem if she didn't get out of my room.

Carey cast a glance around the restaurant. "I wonder if Harriet will come back as a ghost?"

"Hard to say at this point." I lowered my voice, knowing Harriet's death was the number one topic of conversation at the moment. "Since our local Reaper is on strike, though, I'd say the odds are higher here than most places. Let me see the video?"

She turned the laptop around so I could see the screen, and I watched the blurry footage of our visit to Healey House while we ate. At this rate, we'd get more ghost footage if I stuck a camera in my room to record the drama between Mart and our unwelcome visitor, but I wasn't about to tempt either of them to cause even more trouble than they already were. Carey knew more about ghosts than the average person, but that didn't mean she had the years of experience in dealing with ticked-off spirits that I brought to the table.

The next time I looked up, it was to see Detective Drew Gardener enter the restaurant. I waved him over to where we sat, and he strode across the room, mutters following him as he did so.

"Hey, Maura," he said. "Sorry I blew you off yesterday. I didn't expect to run into you out there."

"I know you were working," I said. "I wouldn't have been out if I hadn't been looking for ghosts. The older kind, I mean, not the recent ones."

His serious expression made me aware it probably wasn't the time to joke about that. Dark humour was part and parcel of being around ghosts, though in my experience, most Reapers had no sense of humour whatsoever, dark or otherwise. Yet another reason I had zero desire to join their ranks once again.

Allie approached our table and gave Drew a friendly smile. "Oh, hello, detective. Carey, I need your help with something at the inn. Maura's not working until this afternoon, are you?"

"No," I said, confused as to why she felt the need to point that out. The detective clearly *was* working, and it didn't escape me that everyone else in the restaurant appeared to have noticed him approach our table.

Carey rose to her feet. "Sure. Maura, do you want to take your laptop back?"

"Take it with you." I didn't mind loaning it to her, as she didn't have a computer of her own aside from an ancient desktop Allie had in her office.

Beaming, she packed it back into its case and went out of the restaurant with Casper padding along at her side.

As Allie followed after them, I took the opportunity to step out of the spotlight and headed towards the door leading outside.

Drew fell into step with me. "You're working today, then?"

"Yeah, I'll be on the afternoon shift," I said. "Were you here for a reason?"

"Does there have to be one?"

My heart gave a skip, and I suddenly felt self-conscious of the number of eyes on me. "I wondered if you were here to speak to the people who were at the inn when Harriet drowned. Also, on that note, I have something I need to tell you."

"Oh, sure." He walked with me out of the inn, away from the gossiping witches and wizards, and faced me with a hint of worry in his expression. "What is it? You know something about Harriet's death?"

"No, but I know she died when I was in the old house with Carey." I drew in a breath. "I sensed it, thanks to my Reaper abilities. Maybe half an hour before I saw you on the bridge."

He arched a brow. "You know for certain she died at that moment?"

"It hasn't happened for years, but my senses can't be tricked," I said. "To regular Reapers, it's kind of an automatic compass which tells us where to collect a soul from. My senses aren't as intense as they used to be, but I couldn't have mistaken it for anything else. How long passed between when you were called to the crime scene and when I found you on the bridge?"

"Less than five minutes," he said. "I came as soon as I got the call."

"From one of the wizards?" I asked.

"Yes," he said. "I sent them home after I questioned them about the chain of events which led up to them finding her body. They weren't very coherent, but they clearly didn't know her well, nor did they expect to find a

21

body in the river. They only found her because one of them almost went for a swim himself."

"I gathered, when I saw them talking to you," I said. "I wonder… was she on her way here to the inn? Harriet? I can't think of another reason she might have been on the bridge. There aren't many places open on this side of town that late at night."

"Precisely my thinking," he said. "Which house did you say you were visiting? Was it right next to the river?"

"Healey House." I pointed in the general direction of the sunken old house, nestled between its even more dilapidated neighbours. "There were rumours that ghostly activity picked up over there in the last week or so, but we didn't find anything inside the house. I should have come out as soon as I sensed Harriet's death, but I didn't know it was that close to where I was standing."

"You couldn't tell?" Curiosity underlaid his voice. I hadn't told him everything about being a Reaper, though he'd seen me in action more than once. If I had to admit it, I went out of my way to avoid mentioning it any more than I had to. If there was a time and place to have a long chat about the joys of being tailed by dead people on a daily basis, I had yet to find it.

"No," I said. "For most Reapers, they have a designated area. An entire town or village is generally within reach of their senses, so they have to focus pretty hard to find the right location. It's even worse for me, since my powers have been dormant for… a while. Not much use without a scythe, besides."

It was possible for me to banish a ghost without access to a Reaping tool, but I was way out of practise, and I preferred to keep those situations to a minimum. I could

22

tell when I met Drew's eyes that he was remembering the incident with Mrs Renner, which had seen me go head to head with her ghost and almost lose. Only true Reapers were allowed to wield their tools, and I'd given mine up along with my apprenticeship.

"Sounds like that skill would come in handy when working in homicide," he remarked.

"Not really." I looked down. "I mean, my senses only react when someone is already dead, so it's still too late either way."

"I didn't mean to imply you were in any way responsible for what happened to Harriet," he said. "If anything, I should have been keeping an eye out, since she would have walked straight through pack territory on her way over to the inn."

Drew was a shifter—a wolf shifter, to be precise—as well as being the chief of police, but I doubted there was anything either of us could have done to prevent Harriet's death.

"You couldn't have known," I said. "Are you ruling it an accident, then? Or do you think someone else might have been involved?"

"It's difficult to say at this point."

I was surprised he'd share anything, given how annoyed he'd been when I'd unintentionally barged into the middle of his investigation into Mrs Renner's death when I'd first arrived in town. Okay, I hadn't actually known I was interrupting a murder investigation at the time. I'd been looking for a ghost, that was all. And boy, had the universe delivered.

At first, I'd found the detective as infuriating as he'd found me, mostly due to his getting in my way when I was trying to extract Mrs Renner's ghost. The job had turned out to be more dangerous than either of us had anticipated. In the end, we'd teamed up against said ghost and he'd let me take the lead, while I'd grudgingly accepted his help. From there, we'd ended up… well, I wasn't entirely sure what we were. Friends, sure. I wouldn't say no to working with him again, either.

But I couldn't say for sure that was why I'd entrusted him with the truth about my Reaper senses. Maybe it was just that I wanted to get it off my chest, and he struck me as someone who might understand the misguided sense of responsibility I felt.

It didn't hurt that he was kind, thoughtful and a good listener. That, too. In short, everything I needed in a potential boyfriend, as certain people kept on reminding me. I was a long way from considering pursuing a relationship with anyone, though, let alone the chief of police in a town full of ghosts. And now someone had died, and my Reaper powers were coming back… things had the potential to get complicated. Fast.

On the other hand, I'd like to know where I stood. "Do you need my help, then?"

"I'm not going to ask you to get involved," he said, "but the fact that you were able to sense the time of Harriet's death was a major help. I wouldn't have guessed if you hadn't told me."

"It might be because I was so close to when her body was found," I said. "Are you sure one of those wizards didn't see what happened? Because they arrived at the bridge so soon after she died, you'd think one of them would have spotted her earlier."

"They were drunk enough that I'm inclined to believe

they weren't paying any attention," he said. "I don't believe any of them would have intentionally killed someone, but I intend to question them again, with the added knowledge we have now about the time of Harriet's death."

"Okay." I glanced behind me at the glass doors of the restaurant. "Are they in there?"

"They are," he said. "Want to come with me to speak to them? You can tell me if any of the details don't add up."

I managed to hide my surprise with a raised brow. "Are you sure? I mean, it's not really my business, even if we did work on handling Mrs Renner's ghost together. I'm not really qualified…"

"I've never worked with a Reaper on a case until I met you," he said, "but I might find myself in need of your skills to get in touch with Harriet's ghost, if it turns out there was more to her death than it first appeared. You might have guessed we don't have anyone on staff with that particular talent."

I thought so. Finding her ghost shouldn't be too much trouble, once enough time had elapsed. And I wouldn't deny that it felt good that he trusted me to help him.

"Okay, I'm in," I said.

3

As I'd predicted, all heads turned in our direction when we re-entered the restaurant. Apparently unbothered by the whispers or the attention, Drew made for a group of witches and wizards occupying a table in the corner, drinking copious amounts of coffee and looking more ghost-like than the group of spirits hovering in the opposite corner near the window.

"Bernard." He nodded to a wizard wearing a crooked grey hat and a morose expression. "If it's okay, I'd like to talk to you again about what happened when you found Harriet's body. You said last night that you didn't remember it all."

"I remember seeing her body in the river when Archie nearly fell in," he said. "I levitated her out and realised she was dead."

"Did any of you see her fall in?" he said. "I've recently gained new information which suggests she drowned in the river only minutes before she was discovered."

I twitched, resisting the impulse to butt in. I didn't need to go around broadcasting my Reaper talents for the whole world to hear. Even telling Drew and Carey might backfire on me. If word reached the wrong ears, I might well find the Reaper Council behind me the next time I turned around.

"No," said the droopy red-eyed wizard sitting opposite him, presumably Archie. "We didn't see her until we got on the bridge and looked down into the water."

"Do you think she might have been on her way here?" the detective asked. "When she went across the bridge?"

"Maybe," said Bernard. "I don't know."

"Can I get you anything?" Hayley approached the table with an armful of plates and a set of dark circles under her eyes that matched the patrons'.

"No, thanks," chorused the wizards.

"Give me a shout if you do." She looked pretty subdued herself. No wonder, considering she'd run into a dead body on the way back from work. "Detective, have you spoken to Harriet's ex-boyfriend yet?"

"I didn't know there was one," he said. "Was he here at the bar last night?"

"Who?" said the grey-hatted wizard. "Oh, Maxwell. No, he wasn't. I don't think."

"He wasn't," confirmed his friend. "They broke up a few days ago, right? She was probably still pretty torn up over it all."

"She was in here sobbing the other day," Hayley added. "I saw her. Maybe I should have said something."

"That's news to me," said the detective. "What did you see, if you don't mind my asking?"

Hayley blinked at him. "I just saw her crying in the corner of the bar. Maybe three or four days ago. I didn't say anything, because I figured it was none of my business."

"I saw her, too," added Bernard. "She wasn't alone, though. She was with... what's her face."

"Who?" said Drew.

"I don't know, the blond one."

"Fran," interjected Hayley. "She wasn't here last night, though."

"Hayley!" Allie walked into view. "You look like death. You should have called in sick."

Hayley shook her head. "I know you're understaffed—"

"I have Maura," Allie said, beckoning me over. "You can take over from Hayley for a bit, can't you?"

I hesitated, ready to tell her I was helping the detective with the case, then I remembered that it was unlikely that Harriet's ghost would have shown her face yet. I was supposed to be working later anyway, and there was no harm in starting my shift early. It'd give me something useful to do while I waited for Harriet's ghost to appear. "Sure. I'll let Drew know."

"Oh, I didn't know the two of you had plans."

"We don't." I knew I'd spoken a touch too quickly when her brows rose. "I mean, he's here asking the wizards about the witch who died yesterday."

"And you got curious, did you?" she guessed.

"More or less." I didn't want the whole world to know I could sense when people died. It wouldn't exactly do my non-existent social life any favours. Though the alternative—getting a reputation as a ghost-whisperer—wasn't much better.

Drew approached Allie and me. "Everything okay?"

"I have to take over from Hayley," I told him. "She's pretty shaken up after yesterday."

"No worries," he said. "I'll finish up here, and then I'll need to update the rest of my team. Will I see you later?"

"I'll be working until the evening, but sure," I said. "If you have anything else you want to ask, shoot me a message."

"Will do."

We'd finally exchanged phone numbers—not that I'd made much use of his, since he seemed to be here all the time anyway. I knew Allie was watching our interactions with interest, hoping that he'd finally make a move, but part of me was more than happy to take it slow. Especially now I'd got myself involved in a police investigation thanks to my Reaper skills making a comeback. That alone had enough potential to land me in trouble without bringing my personal feelings into it.

Yet that knowledge didn't mean I could entirely ignore the way my heart lifted at the notion of seeing him later.

———

The restaurant was pretty quiet for most of the day, which worked in my favour, given how tired I was after the ghostly shenanigans I'd had to deal with last night. I loaned Carey my laptop again so she could continue going through footage of the old house, while Mart flew around making sarcastic comments and complaining about the new ghost in my room.

"Now she's in the shower and she won't get out," he whined. "I can't live like this. You can ask Allie to move us to another room, can't you? She'd do it if you asked her, I'm sure."

"I'm not asking to move rooms so I can get rid of a ghost," I told him. "She's not doing any harm."

"Why not just use your Reaper powers to get rid of her, then?" he said.

"Because there might be a reason she picked my room to hide in," I said. "She might need my help, and it's bad manners to kick her out. I'll talk to her after I'm done here."

Mart floated across the restaurant, muttering under his breath. I rolled my eyes after him, checking the time. Ten minutes until the end of my shift.

"Having trouble with ghosts?" said a deep voice. Detective Drew walked into view, having caught the tail end of my discussion with Mart.

"Just my brother," I said. "Want anything?"

"Coffee would be good."

I went to make us both a mug of strong coffee. I was on my fourth, which I'd probably regret tonight when I couldn't sleep, but Mart's antics last night coupled with a long day on my feet had taken their toll. "Late night, was it?"

"I had to escort those drunken wizards home without any of them falling into the river, so yes," he said. "You weren't back too late, were you?"

"Nah, but I had to deal with two arguing ghosts in my room all night." I stifled a yawn. "Occupational hazards of being a Reaper."

"Your brother?"

"And his new nemesis." I made both coffees and carried them to the bar. "A new ghost decided to move into my room and Mart threw a fit. Not sure I wouldn't prefer to deal with Harriet's ghost, to be honest."

"Aside from that, I never asked you how you're getting on with your new job." He took the coffee mug from me and sipped at the dark liquid. "I notice you haven't joined the local coven."

"Covens and I don't get along." My Reaper side made sticking to the rules tricky, and I was better off being independent. Much easier for me and for everyone else, too. Besides, I didn't need a coven. I had everything I wanted already.

Almost everything.

"When does your shift finish?"

He couldn't have picked up on my thoughts, could he? No, he was a werewolf, not a mind-reader. Besides, I'd agreed to help him with the case.

"Not long to go now," I responded. "Did you speak to Harriet's family?"

Why, Maura? If he'd been building up to anything, I'd thoroughly wrecked the mood by bringing up the dead witch.

"I informed her family yesterday," he said. "The funeral is later this week. At the moment, we're ruling her death an accident, though I've let it be known that anyone is welcome to come in and tell me if they have more information. I'm particularly concerned that it seems nobody knew she was out last night. However, I'd rather not distress her family any further by implying her death wasn't an accident. They've dealt with enough in the past day already."

"You mean she might have died by suicide?" I said. "That, or someone pushed her into the water, but everyone said she was alone. If they're telling the truth, that is."

"There's no way to verify that for certain," he said. "Unless…"

"Unless I speak to her ghost."

I'd suspected it might come to that, and while I hadn't wanted to draw attention to my Reaper skills, the fact that I'd felt her moment of death made me reluctant to step away. Besides, I could trust Drew not to tell the entire universe he had a Reaper helping him out. Right?

"Is that okay?" he asked. "I wouldn't ask you to do this if you hadn't suggested it yourself."

"It's no problem," I said. "I talk to ghosts all the time. I can't guarantee she'll show up, but the chances are higher here in Hawkwood Hollow than they would be if we were anywhere else."

"I thought so," he said. "I've spoken to all of Harriet's relations, and I don't get the impression any of them have the ability to see ghosts, nor have they considered the possibility of her returning after death."

"Depends where she shows up, too," I said. "If it's in her own house, alone, then they won't be any the wiser. If it's someone else's house or a public place, it's a different story. My Reaper senses might be able to point me in the right direction, but there are just too many ghosts here in Hawkwood Hollow."

There were ways for a Reaper to track a specific ghost, but most of my old skills were rusty to say the least.

Allie walked into the restaurant from the inn's lobby. "You can sign out, Maura. Oh, hello, Detective."

"Hey, Allie," he said.

"Are you here to take Maura out?" she asked.

"We're off to do a bit of ghost-hunting," I told her. "I'll just go and change first."

I drank the rest of my coffee, then I went upstairs to change into a clean outfit, telling myself that it was courtesy to make the effort to change out of my sweaty work clothes and not that I wanted to look nice when we went out together. Eventually, I settled on a pair of dark leggings and one of my nicest tops. The detective himself wore a shirt and trousers, smart casual wear which indicated he wasn't on duty, though he could snap into work mode when he wanted to. He gave me a smile when I returned to the lobby to meet him. "Ready?"

"Sure." With a little luck, we'd have more luck with this ghost than I had with the last one I'd tried to find.

The two of us walked in companionable silence, the evening air pleasantly cool. I halted on the bridge over the river first, peering down into the murky water. It was deceptively still, and you wouldn't guess that the same river had burst its banks and swamped a huge proportion of the town two decades ago, including Healey House.

"Anything?" he asked. "Is it likely that she'll show up here?"

"Ghosts don't always appear in the place where they died," I said. "Sometimes they show up where they lived, or somewhere they spent a lot of time. That said, it's possible that the ghost might be around here. Her death was recent enough."

I doubted that was the case, though. If she'd been

there, I'd have spotted her right away. Ghosts didn't tend to hang around *in* the water, so she'd have been on the bridge, if at all. I spotted three other ghosts floating down the nearby road, and my gaze followed them.

"More ghosts?" asked the detective.

"You've got it," I said. "I'll see what they have to say."

Leaving the detective on the bridge, I waylaid one of the other ghosts. "Hey. Have you seen Harriet Langley?"

The ghost gave me a wary look. "Who?"

"The witch who drowned yesterday," I said. "I wondered if her ghost might have shown up here."

"No new ghosts," he said. "Are you the Reaper?"

"Not exactly. No, I'm not," I added when he edged away. "I'm not here to reap anyone's soul. Can you let me know if you see her?"

He floated away without answering, but it was obvious no new ghosts had appeared on the bridge. I re-joined the detective, who said, "No luck?"

"Ghosts aren't always that reliable," I said. "I don't think she's here, though."

"I have her address," said the detective. "I also have permission to enter the property from her family."

"That does make it easier." I flashed him a sideways smile. "Easier than swiping a key like in Mrs Renner's house. Guess it pays to have the law on your side."

"It does, but I hope for all our sakes she isn't like Mrs Renner," he said. "She lived alone, according to our records, though she had a boyfriend who moved out fairly recently."

"What, you think she might decide to haunt her friends or family?" I asked. "It's possible, for sure. Depends on how well they got along when she was alive."

We walked the rest of the way across the bridge. I still didn't know my way around the whole town, and the bizarre numbering system on most of the streets didn't help. The road signs seemed to be arranged at random in a lot of places, too, and there were more dead ends and strange detours than the average town. I'd gathered that the randomness was another aftereffect of the floods twenty years ago, which had caused so much destruction that Hawkwood Hollow as a whole still hadn't quite recovered. It didn't help that the Reaper had gone into permanent early retirement, leaving the place flooded with ghosts even after the water had gone.

If my own Reaper instincts came back and started prompting me to banish all of them… that might cause problems. Big ones. I didn't need to be dragged back into an unwanted Reaper career because of my half-Reaper senses refusing to get a hint.

If this particular death was a one-off, though, I needed to know why my senses had chosen to alert me. Which meant going with the detective to speak to Harriet's ghost.

"I think we should check in with the local coven's leader first," he said. "To make sure we aren't stepping on any toes."

"Are you sure?" I asked. "I can't see why she'd forbid us from talking to Harriet's ghost."

"I doubt she will," he said. "But it's best to be certain."

My heart gave an uneasy flip. I hadn't spoken to the local coven leader yet. While it would normally be good manners to introduce myself to her, as a new witch in town, none of the locals had invited me to one of their meetings and most of them outright avoided me. As an outsider, they presumably didn't think I'd be sticking around. Understandable, as I'd never come here intending to stay.

I did my best to quell my misgivings as the detective and I walked up to the large brick house which formed the coven's main base. Like a lot of the buildings in the witches' area of town, it was painted in magenta and mauve shades, while bronze carvings of griffins and unicorns adorned the walls. It stood out next to its relatively bland neighbours, as though the coven leader wanted there to be no doubt where the centre of the coven's finances lay.

Drew walked in through the oak doors and towards a room on the right. A bronze plaque reading, 'Coven Leader: Mina Devlin' was affixed to the door. The detective knocked.

"Come in," said a female voice.

Drew pushed open the door, revealing an office. The woman who sat behind the desk was maybe in her late fifties and wore a long cloak of a deep navy blue. A matching hat perched atop her long curly dark hair, which was streaked with grey, her mouth pulled in a scowl which suggested it was rare for a smile to grace it.

"Detective," said the woman. "To what do I owe the pleasure?"

Her gaze slid to me, and her eyes narrowed. My heart sank a little. I had the sudden suspicion that she knew me by reputation if nothing else.

"I'm here to ask if anyone in your coven has seen Harriet Langley's ghost," he said. "Maura here has the gift of seeing spirits, and she's here to assist me with clearing up the matter of her tragic death."

"I thought you said her death was an accident," said the coven leader.

"Given the circumstances of her death, we can't rule out the possibility that it wasn't," he said. "If her ghost confirms she died by accident, then we can put this behind us. If not, then I may have to reopen the investigation."

"What do you want me to do, perform a summoning spell?" she asked. "I wasn't under the impression that consulting the dead was a standard part of a murder investigation. It hasn't been in the past."

"That's because I haven't worked with someone with the ability to see ghosts before," he said. "Maura here can see and interact with spirits without the need for assistance. While I would be glad to accept your offer under ordinary circumstances, considering the number of ghosts present in Hawkwood Hollow, it's entirely possible that we won't require a spell in order to find her ghost."

I bit back a laugh. The detective and the coven leader clearly had a history of butting heads, since he was employing the same sarcastic tone that he'd used on me when we'd first met. Mina Devlin's expression was cold enough to freeze the river.

"Yes, I hear Maura was involved in the incident in Elizabeth Renner's house," the coven leader said, as if I wasn't standing right in front of her. "Her grandson caused us considerable hassle in the aftermath."

"He left town, though, right?" I'd momentarily forgotten that Mr Renner had tried to pin the blame for his grandmother's house's collapse on the local coven and wanted compensation. Never mind that his own grandmother's vengeful ghost had been the one who'd started all the trouble. That would explain why Mina was inclined to dislike me, though I had the impression she'd have already objected to me purely on the basis of my half-Reaper nature. People like her were sticklers for obeying the rules, and while few witches knew the Reapers' rulebook inside and out, it was common knowledge that Reapers weren't supposed to have affairs with non-Reapers. Much less children. Thanks for that one, Mum and Dad.

"Eventually," she said, her mouth pinching with disdain. "Detective, am I to understand you want this outsider to be involved in an official investigation into one of my fellow witches' deaths?"

"As I explained earlier," he said, "I have nobody on my team with the ability to see or hear ghosts the way Maura can. I need her to act as an interpreter, not an investigator. With your permission, I'd like to go to Harriet's house and see if her ghost has returned following her death."

The coven leader's irritated expression didn't budge an inch. "If you must, go to her house and do as you will. If you want to speak to any of the other members of my coven, then please inform me beforehand."

"Of course," said Drew. "Thank you for your time."

We left our office, not speaking a word until the oak doors of the coven's headquarters closed behind us. I couldn't help noticing there weren't any ghosts inside or outside the building. Maybe the old coven leader had scared them off. It wouldn't surprise me.

I looked at Drew. "If I didn't know better, I'd say she doesn't like me much."

"In my experience of dealing with the coven, she

dislikes most people," he said. "Shall we go to Harriet's house, then?"

"Might as well." I strode alongside him, hiding a grin. "You two have had issues in the past, I can tell."

"You might say that," he said, in disgruntled tones. "Every time a crime so much as carries a hint of the involvement of a coven member, she's there, getting in the way and insisting on taking over the investigation. Most of my team is used to stepping aside by now."

"But you aren't," I observed. "You don't like giving up control."

"Not in the slightest." He led the way into a street lined with terraced houses. "And in this particular case, I happen to think she didn't pay the slightest bit of attention to my report. This is the place."

Harriet's house had a blue-painted door and flowery curtains. Herbs grew in the garden, and rows of potted plants lined the windowsill. She'd worked in the hospital, they'd said, so it made sense that she'd keep her magical herbs here for easy access. The detective unlocked the door and pushed it inward, revealing a white-painted hallway.

"Harriet?" I called.

No response came. My Reaper senses remained quiet, and I shook my head at Drew.

"Nothing?" he asked.

"I can't sense anyone, but I can have a look around." I walked into the first room on the right of the hallway and scanned for any signs of a spiritual presence. None appeared.

As I backed into the hallway, a creak sounded overhead. Someone was upstairs. Living or dead, I couldn't tell.

Pressing a finger to my lips, I climbed the stairs as quietly as I could manage, turned a corner, and spotted a bedroom door half open.

Shadows spread out from my feet as I walked into the room.

4

I trod into the room, keeping my shadows at the ready in case a ghost sprang out and attacked me. Instead, I stepped around the corner and tripped over a solid and very much alive person.

"Hey!" I whipped out my wand, facing the tall muscular man who rose to his feet to stand a foot taller than me. Long blond hair. A shifter, I figured, but not familiar to me in the slightest.

His eyes widened. "Who are you?"

"I could ask you the same question," I said, my heart still pounding in my chest. "You're aware that you're trespassing in Harriet Langley's house, aren't you?"

"So are you," he growled back. "Who even are you?"

"She's working with me," said Drew. "I assume you're the ex-boyfriend?"

The werewolf paled at the sight of the detective. "I just came here to get my stuff. I still have a key, and... and I didn't expect anyone to show up."

"Is that right?" he said. "You didn't assume the police would come here and find you trespassing?"

"No." He backed up a step. "I thought her death was ruled an accident and the police were gonna leave it alone."

"New information has come to light," said the detective.

"Um, like what?" he said. "I wasn't with her when she died. I mean, we haven't seen each other since we bumped into one another at the apothecary three days ago."

"Do you have an alibi for the time of her death?" asked Drew.

"Yes." His shoulders straightened. "I was at home. With my new girlfriend."

That would explain his awkwardness at being found here when his ex-girlfriend had died the previous day. Didn't get him off the hook, though, given the fact that he hadn't exactly acted like an innocent person by creeping around upstairs.

"Is that so?" I said. "And the fact that you hid behind the bed when I came in here wasn't because of a guilty conscience, was it?"

"What?" he said. "No. Who are you? You're not with the police."

"I'm looking for your ex-girlfriend's ghost," I said, figuring I might as well get to the point. "Have you seen her?"

His face went, if possible, even paler. "No. I can't see ghosts anyway, but... no."

"She's not here," said Drew, apparently feeling sorry for the guy. That, or he figured he wouldn't give us any useful information, so we'd be better off getting rid of him. "However, I'm going to ask you to leave. I intended to pay you a visit later this week to question you further, so you'd better prepare to explain yourself."

"I didn't know." He backed into the corridor outside the room. "I swear, I didn't even know she was out that night."

"Then I'd suggest you leave her house." Drew gave him an expectant look.

The werewolf all but shrivelled on the spot. "Um, I'll do that. Bye."

He backed downstairs and out of the house, leaving the two of us alone.

"Guilty conscience?" I queried. "Or was he scared you might shapeshift and terrify him?"

"That, or he saw your shadows."

I looked down at the blackness spilling out from beneath my feet. Oops. "I know I need to work on my people skills."

"You aren't wrong," said Mart.

I gave him a glare, then turned back to the detective. "So does he. He clearly didn't expect to be found here."

"Question is, was he telling the truth?" Drew scanned the room. "I take it there aren't any ghosts in here?"

"Nope, but I'm not sure there were any in the house before that dude showed up." My Reaper senses remained utterly quiet. I gave the room a cursory glance to see if the werewolf had moved anything of Harriet's, but I wouldn't know if anything in the room was out of place. His cover story was plausible enough, and the detective would be able to find out if his alibi for last night held up. Whatever the case, it appeared Harriet's ghost wasn't around. And if she decided to haunt her ex, he wouldn't be able to see her anyway.

By now, it was dark outside, so we left Harriet's house and headed back to the inn.

"Do you think he was just making excuses?" I asked the detective. "Or do you think he'll have something worth saying when you question him later this week?"

"I'll have to speak to my colleagues first, to verify that they're fine with me keeping the investigation open," he said. "Then I'll speak to Maxwell and his new partner tomorrow."

"He's one of the local pack," I said. "Right?"

"He is," he said. "The werewolves are a varied bunch. Some will only date within the pack. Others are more flexible."

Like you? That was a question for another time, because Mart's loud singing from behind my back was a glaring reminder that I had enough problems to deal with. Like the extra ghost in my room, for instance.

"He did say he had a new girlfriend," I said. "Which I gather might have been the reason for their breakup. I got the impression it was recent, anyway, from what I've heard so far."

"So did I," said Drew. "For all we know, her ghost has appeared back at the inn instead."

I hoped not. Two ghosts in my room was already too many for me to handle, thanks.

Drew and I parted ways outside the inn, and I went inside to find Carey sitting behind the desk in the lobby, with Casper prowling around the doorway. He mewed a greeting to me as I walked in.

"Hey," said Carey. "Whereabouts did you end up going?"

"I met the local coven leader, and we didn't exactly hit it off," I replied. "Then we tried to find Harriet's ghost at her house but found her living boyfriend instead. I mean, ex-boyfriend."

Her brow wrinkled. "What was he doing?"

"Getting back his possessions he left in her house, supposedly," I said. "We sent him packing."

Mart snorted behind me. "More like you scared him off."

"Did you?" said Carey. "Why?"

"He wasn't supposed to be there," I said. "Okay, and I don't always make the best first impression."

"Or second," said Mart. "Or third. Or—"

I held up a hand to silence him. "Anyway, we didn't find her ghost, so that was a bust."

"Is your brother there?" she asked, correctly guessing who I was gesturing at. "What's he saying?"

"Tell her about the ghost in your room!" he said.

I weighed up the odds, and then decided that it was worth telling her about the ghost, if just so I might actually get some sleep tonight. "Mart is distressed because another ghost showed up in my room, and he's acting like it's a personal insult to him."

"Another ghost?" she echoed. "Who?"

"She's called Mandy, but she doesn't know how she died or how long she's been a ghost," I explained. "I didn't want to get rid of her without finding out if there's a reason she came after me, but Mart keeps picking fights with her and it's stopping me from sleeping. Anyway, I had to leave her up in my room, so I assume she's still there."

"She won't talk to me either," he said. "It's insulting, really. As though I don't exist."

"Should I come with you to talk to her?" Carey reached for her ghost goggles. "She might remember more now she's been alone for a while."

"That might be an idea," I said. "I don't want to bring out my Reaper skills if I can help it. She might be able to move into a different room if I can convince her to, without needing to ruffle any feathers."

"Just banish her," said Mart. "I don't understand what the problem is."

"I'm not going to start terrorising the local ghosts by reaping their souls," I said, for Carey's benefit as well as his. "We should ask Allie first to make sure she doesn't object to a ghost moving into one of the vacant rooms."

"I'll find her." She ducked out from behind the desk and walked into the restaurant, while Casper rubbed against my legs and purred. He was a personable little familiar, really. Pity about his fear of ghosts, otherwise he'd be good to have around while exploring old houses in search of spirits.

Allie walked into the lobby. "Hey, Maura. Something wrong?"

"Hey," I said to her. "Just having a little ghost-related trouble."

"Is it related to what you and the detective were doing?" Her eyes gleamed with interest.

Honestly. Allie was almost as bad as my brother when it came to her relentless questioning about my non-existent romantic relationship with Drew. Worse, because unlike

Mart, she could be seen and heard by the detective as well as me.

"No," I said. "A local ghost has moved into my room and refuses to leave, but Carey and I will sort her out."

"So what did you and the detective do together?" she asked, unwilling to drop the subject.

"Nothing too exciting," I told her. "We went to talk to the coven leader about Harriet's death. We wanted to see if her ghost showed up, but Mina didn't seem particularly friendly to either of us. She pretty much told us to go away."

"Oh, Mina," she said. "I'm not surprised. She's probably insulted that you implied she wasn't capable of handling the matter herself. She is of the opinion that the coven must handle all its issues within itself and without outside interference."

I'd definitely got that impression from what I'd seen of her. Of course, Allie was a witch herself, so she must know the coven leader better than I did from my first impression. Better than the detective, too.

"Can she see ghosts?" I asked, guessing the answer was 'no'.

"Not as far as I'm aware," she said. "Did she tell you to stay out of the coven's business, then?"

"She said we could go ahead and pay a visit to Harriet's house," I said. "But the detective and I didn't find anyone except for Harriet's ex-boyfriend. Alive, not dead."

"What was he doing?" she said.

"Supposedly collecting his stuff, because he still had a key," I said. "I think the detective wants to talk to him again later in the week, but we couldn't find Harriet's ghost anywhere in the house."

"Might she be haunting someone else?" she asked.

"It's possible," I said. "But with so few people able to see ghosts, I'll probably have to do some poking around, and it depends if the coven leader is cool with that or not. Not to mention I'm not an official investigator."

"You have tomorrow off," she said. "Provided Hayley makes it to her shift, anyway. So you can go with the detective and talk to the ghost. I know he probably won't be able to find anyone else to do it, right?"

"Oh, thanks." *I think.* I'd kind of shoved my way into his investigation and I didn't expect the rest of the police to be any more thrilled about it than Mina Devlin was, but she was right in that the police didn't have a ghost expert on their staff. With the old Reaper's general attitude, I understood why the police had never thought about using the spirits of the dead to obtain evidence before I'd shown up in town. I was starting to understand why the police didn't fraternise with the witches in general, come to that.

"No problem," she said. "Should be quiet tomorrow, I think."

"I might not be out all day," I added. "Depends if the coven leader kicks up a fuss and stops us investigating or not. She doesn't seem to like me much. I guess it's because I didn't introduce myself right away. Are most witches in town part of the coven?"

"There's only one official coven, so the witches who aren't members are independent, like you," said Allie. "Carey and I, too. We have too much going on here at the inn to have time to go to coven meetings. Carey might change her mind when she's older, but for now, she's happy enough without them."

I had to agree. Given my past experience with covens, they could be cliquey and insular, and Carey had to deal with enough of that kind of thing at the witch academy already. Her mother was concerned that her only real friends were her familiar and an ex-Reaper, but on the other hand, it sounded like her fellow witches at the academy were seriously mean. I was definitely not the person to offer advice on dealing with school bullies, but the adult members of the coven I'd met so far hadn't exactly been friendly either.

Not belonging to a coven had never particularly bothered me, but if it turned out I had to play nice with the coven in order to help find out what happened to Harriet, I'd have to grit my teeth and do it. Preferably without accidentally bringing out my Reaper powers and cementing my outsider status even more than I already had.

Carey bounded over, goggles in hand. "Should we go and see the ghost?"

"Sure." I smiled at Allie. "Thanks again for covering for me."

We climbed the stairs and headed up to my room. Mart was nowhere to be seen at first, but he reappeared when we reached the first-floor corridor.

"Are you going to exorcise our unwanted guest?" he said. "It's about time. I can't even go in the room now. I'm stuck out here."

"Come on, Mart." I beckoned to him. "Stop being difficult. You can go into the room. Is she even speaking to you?"

"Does it matter?" he said. "I don't understand why you can't just kick her into the afterlife."

"I can't get my scythe out every time a ghost misbehaves," I said. "If I had one, that is. Also, she hasn't done anything which indicates she might have an above average level of power. She can't even touch or interact with anything. Besides, it's not like this is the first time I've had a ghost in my room who I didn't want there."

"That's cold," Mart informed me.

I rolled my eyes at him and unlocked the door to the room. The ghost sat on my bed, and when she saw us enter, she rose to her feet.

"Is she there?" Carey's gaze followed mine to the bed. She'd adapted to my tendency to talk to invisible people better than anyone else, and she'd grown used to me having conversations with Mart by now. I was still impressed by how quickly she pinpointed the ghost's location.

"Yeah." I pointed at her, and the ghost flinched.

"I don't want trouble," she whispered.

"This is Carey," I told her. "Her mum runs the inn, and she wants to offer you an alternative to staying in my room."

Carey faced the spot where the ghost floated. "My mum and I own this place. We aren't going to make you leave, but we can't let you stay in a guest's room without permission. That said, we have a few empty rooms, if you want to pick one."

"I don't want to be alone." Her voice was small, and it struck me that she'd been younger than me when she'd died.

"Either she goes or I do," said Mart.

"What about the room next door?" I suggested,

ignoring my brother. "It's unoccupied, and if you need my help, you can just come in here and ask for me."

I didn't particularly relish the idea of her floating through the wall in the middle of the night, but it wasn't like Mart didn't do that anyway. Whatever the ghost was frightened of might be a legitimate concern or not, but I needed a decent night's sleep before I passed out on my feet.

"I'll show you into the room," added Carey. "Come with me."

She led the way to the neighbouring room and unlocked the door. I walked that way and beckoned to the ghost. Mandy drifted out of the room, a sad expression on her face.

"My room's right here." I indicated the two doors, and she floated through the one leading to the neighbouring room. "If you need me, give me a shout."

"I will," she said. "Thank you."

Sorted. The ghost had a new corner to haunt, I had my room back, and Mart would have no more reasons to complain.

Famous last words, Maura.

_____

5

While I slept through the night without any ghostly arguments jolting me awake, I woke to the sound of running water. I was too tired to puzzle that one out, so I dozed off for another few minutes. Then I picked up my phone and found a text from Drew asking me to meet him in half an hour. I leapt out of bed and ran around the room pulling on my clothes, then I tugged a comb through my hair. Mart flew into the bathroom as I was brushing my teeth.

"Your ghost friend is causing trouble again," he said in accusing tones.

I rinsed my mouth out. "Huh?"

The sound of running water continued after I turned the tap off. Now I listened more carefully, it was definitely the sound of a shower. Not mine, but the one in the room next door.

Uh-oh. The ghost seemed to have learned how to turn the shower on. Unless Mart had been giving her lessons. I swore, then I ran from the bathroom and grabbed my shoes before slamming into the corridor. Bracing myself, I opened the next room's door to find water seeping underneath the bathroom door and no sign of the ghost.

Suppressing a groan, I trod through the room and pushed open the bathroom door. The ghost had disappeared and left the shower running, and a growing stain covered the carpet in the main room.

I waved my wand and cleaned up the mess in an instant. "Where's the ghost? Mart, have you seen her?"

"No," he said.

I narrowed my eyes. "Are you sure you didn't scare her off?"

He cleared his throat. "That, I can neither confirm nor deny."

I sighed and returned to my own room while Mart flew around in the background, singing, "So long and thanks for all the fish."

When I'd properly gathered my things together, I went down to the lobby. Carey looked at me from the desk when I hurried into view. "Something wrong, Maura?"

"The ghost flooded the bathroom in the room next door to mine," I said. "Don't worry, I cleaned it up."

"I didn't know she could do that," she said.

"Nor did I," I said. "She didn't have that much power at her disposal at first, but maybe she was unaware of her own strength. Personally, I want to blame Mart. Either he taught her to do it, or he did it himself and let her take the blame so I'll get rid of her."

"Ah." Her brow wrinkled. "Is she still in the room now?"

"No, but she'll be back, no doubt," I said. "Given how scared of everyone she seems to be. I'm meeting Drew in a few minutes, so I have to go, but I'll be back to check on her later."

I hurried into the restaurant to grab a piece of toast to eat on the go before the detective arrived and returned to the lobby as Allie took over the desk from her daughter.

"Maura, what's wrong with the ghost?" she asked.

"Reading between the lines, Mart scared her off," I said. "Pretty sure he turned on the shower and flooded the place, too. He won't admit it, but I cleaned up the mess anyway."

"Thanks, Maura," she said. "Whereabouts is the ghost now?"

"I have no idea," I said. "I'd look for her, but the detective will be here any minute now. I can tell him to go ahead without me—"

"No, you can't miss out on time with the detective." Her eyes twinkled. "I'm sure the ghost won't do any lasting damage."

I hope not. It was a good job the water hadn't leaked onto the floor below or caused any more damage to the carpet. Mart himself was conspicuously absent, so I busied myself with eating my toast while I waited for the detective to arrive.

I drank the last of my coffee, spotted the detective approaching the doors, and went out to meet him.

"Everything okay?" asked Drew.

"More or less," I said. "My new ghostly friend learned how to turn on the shower overnight and keeps arguing with my brother, but at least she isn't in my room anymore."

"You still haven't got rid of her yet?" he asked. "Who is she, anyway?"

"She calls herself Mandy, and she's terrified of everything and thinks I can protect her." I rolled my eyes. "Also, I blame my brother for teaching her the trick with the shower. He's a menace."

"I hope you're still up for coming with me to talk to Maxwell again today," he said.

"Sure thing." I did my best to put the ghost out of mind, hoping that Allie would find a solution while I was gone. "I'll resume the ghost-hunting when I come back to the inn."

For now, it was time to pay a visit to Harriet's werewolf ex-boyfriend and his new partner. I hoped he'd be more helpful than he'd been yesterday, though it was anyone's guess as to whether either of them would admit to being haunted by his ex's ghost.

The detective and I walked back to the same district we'd visited yesterday, stopping in a cul-de-sac near a park and heading down a row of terraced houses.

"This is still in the area where the witches live, right?" Werewolves tended to prefer to live closer to the woods, where they could freely shift between animal and human forms without causing a fuss.

"It is," he confirmed.

"He already moved in with her?" I said. "Didn't he and Harriet just break up like a week ago?"

"Werewolves don't do things by halves, generally."

No kidding. "Speaking from experience?"

Oops, I probably shouldn't have said that aloud. Luckily, Maxwell chose that moment to answer the door. The tall blond werewolf greeted the detective with an expression which looked as though he expected to face a short walk to the gallows.

"Detective," he said, his throat bobbing nervously. "Do come in."

"We can do the interview here, if you like," he said. "I just want to ask you a couple of questions about your whereabouts when Harriet died."

"I was here, at home," he said. "Lisa can back me up."

"And did the two of you speak at all on the day of her death?" asked the detective.

"No," he said. "Like I said, the last time we spoke to one another was when we bumped into each other at the apothecary the other day. We didn't speak much. I think she was as embarrassed as I was."

"Do you know why Harriet would have been on the bridge at the time of her death?" Drew queried.

"I guess she might have been on her way to the bar at the inn," he said. "We used to go there together."

Hmm. I'd need to check in with Allie and the other regulars if I wanted more detail on how often Harriet had been seen in the bar in the last week. "Would she have been walking on her own in the dark?"

"I don't see why not," he said. "The town's generally pretty safe. Everyone knows one another, and I imagine she was probably planning to meet up with someone there."

"Who were her particular friends, do you know?" I probably should have asked the wizards in the restaurant yesterday. "I mean, the people she would have met with?"

"Fran something or other… they used to be friends, anyway," he added. "Not sure they still are. I mean, were, before she died."

"Oh?" I said. "What do you mean?"

He chewed his lower lip. "Some coven drama. Not

sure. I'm not in the coven—obviously—and I wasn't involved in that part of her life."

Sounds like a great foundation for your relationship. I'd be a hypocrite to say so aloud, though. Most of the relationships I'd had had been short-lived, after all, and full of too many secrets to work long-term.

"Not at all?" said Drew. "Is that why you left?"

"It wasn't—I didn't mean to hurt her," he said. "Lisa and I just have more chemistry, and we're made for each other. Know what I mean?"

I was starting to regret even starting this conversation. "Is she home now?"

"Yeah, she is."

It would have been nice to know that earlier.

"Can we speak to her?" asked the detective.

"Sure, I'll get her." He retreated into the house and I heard him climbing the stairs and calling out Lisa's name.

After a moment's pause, Lisa descended the stairs. Tall and dark-haired, she bore more than a passing resemblance to the photos I'd seen of Harriet and was clearly a witch, too. I was starting to get the impression the werewolf had a type.

"Detective," she said. "You wanted to speak to me?"

"I just wanted to ask you a couple of questions," he said. "Whereabouts were you the night of Harriet Langley's death, two days ago?"

"Here, at home," she said promptly. "With Maxwell."

"Did you know Harriet?" I asked.

"I didn't know her personally, but she seemed nice enough," said Lisa. "She was one of the few coven members who was nice to those of us who chose not to join and didn't go out of her way to avoid us."

"Really?" I said. "I heard she had some drama with someone else in the coven…"

"Who didn't?" she said. "The coven thrives off drama."

"They do," added Maxwell. "Look at how they reacted during the conflict over the coven healer position. Who got it in the end, Cathy?"

"I wasn't there, and neither were you," she said. "It's not nice to make assumptions."

"I'm not," he protested.

"Who's Cathy?" asked Drew.

"She works at the hospital," said Maxwell. "Same place Harriet worked. Have you found her ghost yet?"

"No." I didn't see or sense any ghosts in their house, either, but I couldn't picture Maxwell or Lisa being involved in anything nefarious. Drew asked a couple more questions, and then our interview drew to a close.

The detective nodded. "All right, thanks for helping us out."

We turned our backs on the house and walked away, out of the cul-de-sac and around a corner.

"So… the hospital," Drew said. "Do you think it's worth looking there for Harriet's ghost?"

"Hospitals are the worst places for runaway spirits." I shuddered. "I always get mobbed when I set foot in one. Not sure if her ghost would show up in a crowded place like that."

"If that's the case, we're better off speaking to more witnesses," he said. "I wonder what they meant by coven drama?"

"You think I know?" I frowned. "I guess Mina Devlin probably knows everything that goes on among her coven members, but I doubt she'll be forthcoming."

"Not to me," he said. "Mina said she prefers people to go through her if they want to talk to the other witches who are members of the coven, though. They're quite resistant to outsiders trying to get in, including other paranormals."

My brows shot up. "Wait, you think she's more likely to talk to me than to you, because I'm a witch?"

"Exactly," he said. "If you get in her good graces, you might be able to talk to Harriet's friends and see if their conflicts were serious enough to be worth further consideration."

"I don't know if they'd be willing to talk to me," I said. "You might have gathered I'm not a people person."

"It's worth a shot," he said. "The coven holds meetings two evenings a week. If you go there and talk to them, you might get information you wouldn't hear through an interrogation."

I shook my head. "I'm not a coven member. I'm only half-witch, and I haven't been to a coven meeting in years. I definitely haven't paid attention to any of the current events that'll be of interest to other witches in town."

"That doesn't matter," he said. "You're new in town. Every newbie gets to attend a trial meeting while they're taking their time to decide whether to join the local coven or not. I can't think of a better way to get an impression of what might be going on with the other members."

Unfortunately, neither did I. "When do they meet?"

"There's a meeting tonight, in fact," he said. "We could check in with Mina on the way back and see what she says."

I caved. "All right, I'll check it out, just as a one-off."

I'd only be able to use the newbie excuse once, and

given my past experiences in coven meetings, the odds of this going badly were higher than ideal. Witches were even more unwelcoming to outsiders than Reapers, in my experience. On the other hand, what better way to question everyone who knew Harriet without them suspecting I was trying to contact her ghost?

I just had to keep my Reaper skills under wraps for one night. That was all.

6

"You're going to a coven meeting?" My brother cracked up laughing, rolling around in mid-air. "Have you been to a single one since you left home?"

"No." In fact, I was pretty sure I hadn't attended any coven meetings since before Mart's untimely death. When I'd first started training as a Reaper, my mother had attempted to drag us both to regular meetings with the local witches in order to change our minds, but both of us were stubborn and had our hearts set on the Reaper path.

Mart had had it easier than I did. Witch coven leadership was typically matriarchal, while the wizards tended to take a back seat, mostly by choice. That meant I'd been the one to deal with all the comments about how I was letting my family down by not opting to help my mother run the village's leading witch coven. It was perhaps odd that a career in Reaping had been more appealing to me, but in my experience, coven witches could be scheming and downright brutal compared to the Reapers, and older witches were just as petty and immature as the kids at the academy when they wanted to be.

"Good luck." Mart floated along behind me as I picked up speed to catch up with the detective. "I'll come in and laugh at you if I get bored."

"Glad to have your vote of confidence." I caught up with Drew and we turned the corner on the way to the coven headquarters. "Mart is not winning any prizes for being a supportive sibling."

"Isn't he?" he said. "What's he doing?"

"Promising to laugh at me when I go to the coven meeting," I said. "I'd like to say it won't be that bad, but given how Mina treated me last time we spoke, I'm not expecting a welcome party."

I'd be lucky if she didn't show me the door there and then when the coven found out about my Reaper history. Could I get through a meeting without the subject coming up? Well, that depended on how far the rumours about the debacle at Mrs Renner's house had spread.

Bracing myself, I entered the witches' headquarters and knocked on Mina's office door. A moment passed before she called, "Come in."

I entered. The coven leader sat at her desk, same as before, and regarded me with an expression of absolute disdain.

"You again?" she said.

"Hey," I said. "I'm here to ask if it's okay if I attend the coven meeting tonight."

"Why do you need to ask?" she said. "Anyone new to the town can come. Any witch, that is."

I didn't miss the emphasis she put on the word *witch,*

as though to imply she was well aware I was half... not-witch. So much for avoiding issues with my Reaper side.

"I just thought I'd be polite," I said, trying to keep my tone friendly. "See you later."

I left the office and closed the door behind me. Then I re-joined the detective and we left the coven headquarters.

"No problems?" he said.

"Except her attitude, no. I hope the others aren't as bad." Given what I'd seen so far and heard about the coven's members as a whole, though, I had my doubts they'd be welcoming to a half-Reaper with a reputation as a troublemaker. Still, if I wanted to get answers, I'd just have to grin and bear it.

"With any luck, this'll be a one-off," he said. "I appreciate you helping me out."

"No worries." The warmth inside me at his words almost made up for my dread at having to face a coven of witches in which I'd be the unquestionable outsider.

Almost.

———

It was with some trepidation that I returned to the witches' area of town later that evening. I'd spent longer than usual picking out my outfit, opting for a flowery top and skirt rather than my usual dark, unobtrusive ghost-hunting gear. I even dusted off my only hat—literally, because I hadn't worn it in several years—and put on my most witchy cloak so nobody would doubt that I belonged there. Tonight, I was all witch, not a Reaper.

"You missed a cobweb," Mart told me as I walked out of the inn.

I gave my hat another shake before repositioning it atop my head. "Better?"

My brother floated beside me. "You look like you're on your way to a Halloween party."

"Perfect." I left the inn behind and headed across the bridge, holding my hat with one hand to keep it from blowing away. "That's exactly what I'm going for."

"You want to impress Mina Devlin?" He snorted. "Personally, I'd use an earplug charm if you want to get through this meeting without strangling anyone."

"That won't win me any friends, Mart."

He had a point, though. Coven meetings tended to consist of several hours of listening to witches who loved the sound of their own voices arguing about inane things like whether to build a new broomstick-only cycle lane or change the standard coven uniform from blue to grey. Most of the time, I couldn't even pretend to be interested, but for the sake of learning the truth about Harriet's death, I was willing to give it a try. If nothing else, I'd stay for the chance to socialise with the others and learn how things worked here among the witches of Hawkwood Hollow.

I made my way to the witches' headquarters again, crossing my fingers that I wouldn't be the first or the last to arrive, and headed for the designated coven meeting room. Twenty or thirty chairs filled the room, half of which were full already, and all heads turned in my direction when I walked in.

Then the whispers started. A witch wearing pink

leaned over to speak to her neighbour. "She really did show up, then."

"Thought she was a Reaper," responded her friend.

That didn't take long.

I was used to the stares and the whispers, so I ignored them and took a seat on the end of a row, just far enough away that I was within reach of the door without being pegged as antisocial. Maybe I should have taken Mart's advice and cast an earplug charm on myself after all, so I didn't have to listen to them gossiping about me.

The other witches filed into the room in groups until almost every seat was taken. They were an eclectic bunch, ranging from young to old, and most wearing some variety of the typical cloak-and-hat attire. At least I'd gone in the right direction with my fashion choices, but looking like one of them didn't stop the whispers and judging stares. I might as well be a hare among rabbits.

Never mind the earplug charm. I should have just magicked myself invisible and sneaked in as a spy instead. Not that it was likely I'd have got away with it, considering the coven's sharp-eyed leader.

Mina Devlin walked to the front of the room and faced the other witches. Her gaze flickered to me, and I fixed on a false smile until she looked away.

"We have a new guest with us today," she said. "This is Maura."

"Hello, Maura," chorused the coven members.

Now they weren't even pretending not to stare at me. Their expressions ranged from mildly curious to assessing wariness, as though they thought I might pull out a scythe in front of everyone. *This is going well.*

"Hello," I said to the assembled witches. "I'm new in

town, but I've had a hectic few weeks so far and this is the first time I've had the chance to come and attend a coven meeting. I hope that's okay."

"No, it isn't," said the older witch wearing pink attire, one of the witches I'd seen whispering about me. "We don't want newbies."

"She's joking," said her friend, an equally elderly witch wearing a mauve cloak and hat. "I heard you were a Reaper."

Whispers spread among the witches like an infectious rash, as though they hadn't already discussed the matter while they'd been entering the room.

"I'm half-Reaper, but I live as a witch." Aside from the ghosts who regularly showed up in my life, that was more or less true.

"Is that why you have a spider on your hat?" asked the older witch.

Everyone else cracked up laughing, while I found myself hoping a ghost would float in so I could excuse myself to go and do Reaper things without bothering with this nonsense. Even if that would only draw more unwanted attention. Instead, I gave a weak chuckle, though their sense of humour left much to be desired.

After the novelty had worn off, the witches turned to the issue of the day: Seven Millimetre Boots.

"They oughtn't have legalised them," said the pink-clad witch, who turned out to be called Marie. "We can't have young witches zipping around the countryside."

"You did that all the time when you were younger," her friend pointed out. "Before they banned Seven-League Boots."

"Pity, that."

The room dissolved into bickering, while I found myself wishing I'd used an earplug charm from the start. Or at least planned an excuse to get out without offending everyone and winding up on Mina Devlin's bad side. Mart floated through the wall every few minutes to pull faces and otherwise clown around, but even he got bored eventually. I found myself wishing I'd scheduled an evening of ghost-hunting with Carey instead. Exploring a damp, flood-damaged house in search of lost spirits would be preferable to listening to another of Marie's anecdotes about her exploits as a young witch with too much time on her hands.

The blond witch on my right-hand side seemed as eager to get out as I was. She kept fidgeting and looking at the door, and when the elderly witch called her to attention, she jumped.

"Falling asleep there, Fran?" queried Marie.

"Leave her alone, Marie," her friend admonished. "She's had a difficult week."

Fran... the name rang a bell. Hadn't she been Harriet's friend? If she'd dragged herself to a coven meeting expecting them to pay any attention to her plight, it seemed she'd come to the wrong place.

After the meeting finally dragged to a halt, the coven members voted to head down to a pub around the corner called the Crooked Broomstick. The dingy place smelled vaguely of mould underneath the potent smell of the magical cocktails which filled glittering glasses behind the bar, while damp covered the walls. Overall, the place looked as though it'd been dredged up from under the river after the flood without being restored to its former state. No fewer than eight ghosts occupied the bar, but the witches crowded in without paying any heed to their ghostly companions.

Marie bought a round of strong cocktails for the rest of the coven and started dropping loud hints that she wanted to hear everyone sing karaoke. A raised platform in the corner seemed to be designated for that purpose, but when one of the pimply teenage staff members spoke into the microphone, the buzz of static made everyone cringe.

At least the cocktails gave me something to do with my hands and helped me get closer to becoming blissfully unaware of how out of place I was for a bit. I spotted Fran sitting alone at the bar, her blond head drooped over her neon pink cocktail glass. Maybe I wasn't the only person who felt like I didn't belong here.

"Hey," I said to her. "I'm—"

"Maura, I know." She sniffed. "Not to be rude, but I've had a rough week, and I would like to be left alone."

"I get that." I cast my mind around to find a reason to talk to her about Harriet without causing distress. "I'll buy the next round."

"Hear that?" said old Marie in a carrying voice. "She just offered to buy us a drink."

"I'll take three," called one of the other witches.

Great. It seemed I'd discovered the secret to gaining goodwill among the rest of the coven... spend an eye-watering amount on sparkling magical cocktails.

At once, the whole atmosphere turned friendlier, and Fran didn't object to me taking a seat next to her. Two drinks later and she was talking openly to me about the countrywide Sky Hopper championships. Now that was more my speed, but I just knew that mentioning Harriet would bring our conversation to a screeching halt. I was not exactly socially adept when it came to dealing with people who *didn't* see the dead on a regular basis, much less when it came to discussing such matters in a way that wouldn't cause them to ostracise me.

Just when I was starting to grasp at straws to figure out a way to bring up her friend, Fran called to the others.

"Let's have a toast to Harriet," she said.

"To Harriet." A dozen glasses clanked against one another, and a solemn atmosphere descended upon the gathering witches. I noted that Mina Devlin had neglected to attend this part of the meeting, though mercifully, the staticky noise from the microphone had died down somewhat.

Fran gave a loud sniff. "I can't believe she's gone."

"I heard." I put on a gentle tone. "I'm so sorry. Let me know if there's anything I can do for you."

Her eyes brimmed over. "It's so—sudden. I never expected it."

A red-haired witch put a comforting arm around her as she conjured a handkerchief and sobbed into it.

"It's such a tragedy," said Angela, Marie's friend, who'd taken a seat on the other side of me. "She had her whole life ahead of her."

"I heard there was some kind of drama before her death," I said delicately. "In the coven, I mean."

She scoffed. "They do love to gossip, don't they? Who told you that?"

"Um, I work at Allie's restaurant and inn," I explained. "There's a group of wizards who hang out there. They're the ones who found her body, so rumours started to spread the day after the incident."

"Wizards?" she said. "Oh, *them.* They got jealous of our coven and decided to start their own to spite us. It wouldn't surprise me if they started rumours to give all of us a bad name."

"Would they really spread rumours about someone who died, though?" I said. "I'd have thought that would be in poor taste."

She leaned in. "If they said anything about Fran and Harriet arguing, Harriet told her she didn't appreciate her romantic advice. That's all. Her death was a tragic accident, and that's all there is to it."

I finished up my cocktail. By now, I was feeling slightly unsteady on my feet, though not as much as Marie, who tried to stand up to do karaoke and then fell asleep on the stage, there and then. Two staff members escorted her from the premises, while I began gathering my own excuses to leave. I'd done quite enough mingling for one day, and if I drank one more cocktail, I'd never remember anything they told me anyway.

"Marie always overdoes it," said Angela, shaking her head. "Cathy is going to love that. She's on the night shift again."

Wait. I knew that name. "Who's Cathy?"

"New coven healer," said the witch. "She works at the hospital, same place Harriet used to work."

"I heard they used to be friends, too," I said carefully.

Fran scoffed. "Before Cathy stole the position of coven healer out from underneath her, maybe."

Was that the source of the drama? "Stole? What does that mean?"

"It means Cathy was scheming against her from the start," said Fran in a thick voice. "The two of them both had their sights set on the new position of healer, and now Harriet's ended up dead. I bet Cathy's glad of it."

"Fran, stop it," her red-haired friend admonished.

"Does it matter?" She hiccoughed. "She's not here. Not anymore."

"Is there only one coven healer, then?" I turned to Angela.

"There is," she replied. "When old Angie retired, both Cathy and Harriet wanted the spot, but Cathy already got the job before Harriet died, fair and square. Mina herself chose her."

I looked around for the coven leader and saw no signs of her, confirming that she must have left early. For once, I didn't blame her. There was definitely something odd going on among the witches, but it might just be typical coven shenanigans. Would they really commit murder over whoever wanted the job as the coven's healer? Maybe, but the victim hadn't even got the job, so it seemed irrelevant.

In the meantime, it was clear I wasn't going to get any more sense out of anyone, so I made my excuses and left the pub, swaying with each step.

By the time I got back to the inn, I was in dire need of a good night's sleep, preferably without any ghosts interrupting me. Instead, I found a group of drunken wizards being escorted from the inn by an irate Hayley.

"Go on, shoo," she said. "And please try not to fall into the river on the way back."

I ducked around the group as they left, grumbling amongst themselves. My own steps were a little unsteady, too, and I waved at Hayley on the way in.

"Damn those cocktails," I said. "Marie can drink me under the table and she's three times my age."

"You were at the coven meeting?" she said, sounding surprised.

"Yeah, I thought I'd check it out," I said. "Ended up needing a drink or three to make it bearable. Are you a member of the coven?" Given her absence at the meeting, I'd guess not, but I'd assumed attendance wasn't mandatory.

"No," she said. "I left a few years ago, and I doubt I'll be going back."

"Nor me." I'd leave the detective work to Drew in the future, thanks. And the drinking, too, because it seemed I was more of a lightweight than I remembered. Then again, those cocktails were no joke.

Allie waited in the reception area with her arms folded across her chest. "There you are, Maura."

I frowned. "What's up?"

"That ghost of yours," said Allie.

Oh, no. That's what I got for leaving her alone for the evening. "What's she done now?"

"I assume she's the one who stripped off all the bedsheets in her room?"

"That might have been Mart," I said. "Sorry I wasn't around. I'll go and look for her now."

At least I wasn't too drunk to climb the stairs, though I had to hang onto the handrail for balance at the tight corners.

"Had fun at the meeting, did you?" said Allie, with some amusement.

"Nope." I pushed off the wall and approached my

room. "I think I'd rather have dealt with the ghost instead."

She chuckled. "I can't say we didn't warn you. Are you going to have to banish her?"

"I'd rather not," I said. "If just because it'll freak out the other ghosts in the area. Then we can say goodbye to ever turning this place into a haunted hotel."

"You can do that, though?" she asked. "Make her leave?"

"Yeah, but I don't like using my Reaper powers on ghosts who haven't done anything to deserve being forced out," I said. "Besides, most spirits here in Hawkwood Hollow are probably used to being allowed to stick around. I don't want a reputation among the others."

"You think all the ghosts will be afraid of you?"

"It happens." It had never really bothered me before, but the coven meeting today had hammered home how woefully out of touch I was with the magical community at large. I didn't need to alienate the town's ghostly population as well as the living one. "I don't want to rock the boat. Also, I'm pretty sure I'm not sober enough to pull off a banishment without something going awry."

I didn't need to accidentally introduce everyone in the building to the afterlife, for instance. Though it might have brought a bit of excitement to the coven meeting.

"Fair enough," said Allie. "Let me know if you need me."

I entered the ghost's room, where all the covers had been stripped from the beds and slung around the room. Scanning for the ghost, I found her hiding behind a curtain made of bedsheets. When I spotted her, she yelped and clutched the sheet, only for her hands to pass right through it.

"What are you doing in here?" I tried to keep my tone gentle. "Why'd you strip off the bedsheets?"

"I didn't mean to," she whispered. "I heard loud voices downstairs, and I got scared."

"Scared of what?" I pressed.

She shook her head. "The noise just frightened me, that's all."

"All right, I'm going to fix the room." I took out my wand and returned the covers to the bed. As I fixed up the place, she remained huddled in the corner, then slowly straightened upright.

"Thanks for checking on me," she whispered.

"No worries," I said. "Next time, if you need me, just ask. And please don't turn the shower on, okay?"

I backed out of the room and closed the door.

"Everything okay?" asked Allie.

"More or less. I don't think she means any harm."

Yet there was definitely something not quite right about that ghost, not least of which was her sense of timing. But until I figured out what her deal was, I wouldn't be banishing her.

"What's her problem?" Mart wanted to know.

"Weren't you watching her?" I asked. "You didn't come to the Crooked Broomstick."

"That's because the meeting bored me to death," he said. "If I wasn't already dead, I mean. I got fed up waiting for you to make a fool of yourself and sing karaoke, so I went for a walk."

That figured. I turned around to face Allie. "Do you

know what might have upset her? She mentioned hearing noises…"

"The singing downstairs, perhaps," she said. "The wizards always go over the top on coven meeting nights. If anyone here could see ghosts, I'd have one of them keep an eye on her."

I paused. "I do have someone who can, but he's not going to like it."

"What?" said Mart. "Why are you looking at me like… oh, no. Absolutely not."

"Sorry, Mart," I said, "but you're the only one I trust to do this."

Allie smiled, understanding. "Your brother will watch her?"

"No, he won't!" Mart howled.

"Yes, he will." I gave him a stern look. "I'm sure we can come to an agreement."

"No," he said flatly.

"I'll give you access to my shower for an hour."

"No."

"Every day for a week."

"No."

"I'll watch every single old *Doctor Who* episode with you."

"No."

"And all the Star Wars movies. Including the prequels."

He groaned. "And what? What do you want me to do?"

"All you have to do is watch the ghost when I'm not around and let me know if she's causing trouble," I said. "Nothing too strenuous."

He gave a deep, heavy sigh, as though he had the

weight of the world on his transparent shoulders. "I *suppose* I could make the sacrifice for you."

"Also," I added, "if I find out you're the one turning the shower on in her room, then I'll let her move back in here instead."

He moaned and whined and generally made a nuisance of himself, but I was so tired that I passed out cold in the middle of his tirade.

———

The following morning brought me a message from Drew while I was preparing for my shift at the restaurant. I'd taken a hangover potion to get rid of the effects of the night's adventures, which I was glad of, considering Mart was still in a huff and floating around muttering to himself behind my back.

I went to meet the detective in the lobby, my heart lifting at the sight of him despite my lingering bad mood from the previous night.

"How was the coven meeting?" asked Drew.

I pulled a face in answer.

"That bad?"

"You have no idea," I said. "The witches argued for nearly an hour about magical shoe regulations and then I had to follow them to the pub to get a chance to talk to anyone, which ended with me having to pay for an entire round of expensive neon cocktails and listen to Marie's singing."

"Next time, send me a message and I'll come and rescue you."

"I'll keep that in mind," I said. "In fairness, the cocktail thing was my idea, and it was probably the only way I could get them to talk to me about Harriet."

"Did you find out anything?" he asked.

"Not much of note." I thought back. "I met Fran, Harriet's friend, and confirmed that the two of them argued before her death, but it sounds like Fran was trying to give Harriet unwanted romantic advice on the situation with her ex. Not sure that's a motive for murder. She seemed pretty torn up about Harriet's death."

"So she hasn't seen her ghost, I assume," he said.

"No, but apparently, Harriet had her heart set on becoming the coven's new official healer after the last one retired, and ended up losing the position to someone called Cathy," I said. "Fran was hopping mad on her behalf and throwing around accusations, but she was also pretty drunk, so I'm not sure if it's worth checking out."

"Cathy works at the hospital, same as Harriet," he said. "Her name's already come up a couple of times. Is that all?"

"Yeah." At the expectant look on his face, I kind of wished I'd been bolder with my questions. "I didn't get a complete picture of the coven from one night."

"You did great," he said. "Thanks."

His words warmed me inside. "I should go and get ready for my shift."

"When do you finish?"

"Mid-afternoon," I responded.

"If that's the case, then I'll see if I can get us permission from the coven leader to speak to Cathy at the hospital this afternoon," he said. "I'm keeping the investigation open for now."

"Good thinking." Even if Cathy turned out to be innocent, speaking to her might unearth more details about Harriet and help us to fill in the gaps around what happened to her the night of her death. Learning more about this coven healer business would be a good start. As a bonus, anything that didn't involve another coven meeting was more than okay in my book.

"It's up to you if you want to come," he added. "I know Mina is unlikely to be thrilled, and if you'd prefer not to risk getting on her bad side, you can sit this one out."

"Nah, I'm pretty sure our friendship is a lost cause already." I wouldn't object to the notion of getting to spend more time with the detective, and besides, maybe the new healer could shed some light on what was really going on in the coven.

7

F irstly, I had to get through another shift at work. The restaurant was fairly quiet while Carey was at school, and Mart had gone to sulk in my room after he'd got bored with flying around being dramatic and complaining about the ghost's presence next door. That gave me time to think on what I'd learned at the coven meeting last night. Aside from everything it was possible to know about the local witches' views on magical boots and broomstick regulations, that is.

I brewed up a second hangover cure as my headache began to return, wondering what had possessed the coven to hold their meeting on a Monday night. Carey's mother walked into view as I tipped it into a mug.

"Those coven witches can really drink, can't they?" said Allie. "Sorry I dragged you upstairs to deal with the ghost when you'd already had a day of it."

"No worries." I finished making the hangover cure and took a long sip. "Mart's keeping an eye on her. Anyway, the after-party was the best part of last night, and that's not saying much."

"You went to the Crooked Broomstick?" she asked.

"Yeah," I said. "Ended up dealing with Fran sobbing over her friend's death and throwing accusations around, and old Marie being escorted from the premises for drunkenly falling asleep during karaoke."

"And then you came back here to find Hayley doing the same to those wizards." She shook her head. "Menaces, they are."

"Are they always that bad?" I drank the rest of the mug's contents in two big gulps.

"Unfortunately," she responded. "They seem to have taken it upon themselves to be their own coven in all but name, but with zero discipline or leadership. Was it worth going to the meeting, then?"

"I know more about the hazards of Seven Millimetre Boots now," I said. "Other than that... not really."

"I gathered." She tilted her head. "I assume it had nothing whatsoever to do with the detective asking you to speak to the coven as a favour, did it?"

Busted. "I'm a witch and he isn't, so he asked if I could drop by a meeting to get some useful information on Harriet. Seemed easy enough in theory."

"But it didn't work out?"

I shrugged. "I did learn that Harriet was trying out for the position of coven healer not long ago but didn't get it. Who was the last coven healer?"

"Angie retired last week," she said. "She still works at the local apothecary, but she's officially retired from coven duties, so it makes sense that the coven would have recently brought in a replacement. I'm surprised she stayed in the job for so long, given how ungrateful Mina is known to be to her staff."

I turned this information over in my mind. It might be worth speaking to Angie next, as well as her replacement, if I wanted to learn how this coven healer business operated. I made a mental note to tell the detective and busied myself with the tasks of the day.

When Carey came back from school, she brought her homework into the restaurant and claimed her usual table to work at near the bar, where we could talk to one another easily.

"I think we should go back to Healey House this weekend," she said. "It's worth having another look around. Sometimes ghosts can vanish and then reappear later on, right?"

"They can." Perhaps it was worth heading back, given how distracted I'd been while we'd been exploring the old house the first time around, but I'd rather leave it until after the detective and I had finished looking into Harriet's death. The old house sat too close to the river for my liking.

"I haven't posted anything new on my blog in days," she admitted. "I think my readers are getting fed up with me posting videos of your brother levitating things and switching lights off to make up for any actual ghost-hunting missions."

"Better not tell him that," I said. "He's more sensitive than he lets on, and he's having a challenging week."

"Because of the other ghost?" she guessed. "How about we ask them to do a double act?"

"Not sure Mart would like that idea either," I said. "Mandy definitely wouldn't. She hates attention."

She nodded. "Oh, of course. I don't want to upset her. I was thinking, though, about your idea of using the ghosts to advertise the inn…"

"Depends how many people like the idea of a screaming ghost keeping them awake all night," I said. "Mandy would fit the bill if she wanted to haunt anyone except for me, but half the attraction of a haunted hotel is knowing who the ghosts were when they were still alive. We don't know who she is, not really."

"Yeah, we need to find out her story if we want her to help us run a ghost tour," she said. "You never know, though. Her friends might follow."

"Hopefully not into my room." Mostly for Mart's sake. He was still sulking somewhere and avoiding me, and I owed him for keeping an eye on the ghost as it was.

This was precisely why I'd stopped being a Reaper, even on an unofficial basis. Things just got way too complicated whenever the dead were involved. One minute I'd been helping a ghost, the next I was stuck at a coven meeting listening to witches argue about shoes. Admittedly, it was *possible* the detective had had more to do with that particular decision than my compulsion to get involved with ghosts, but still. The new spirit next door to my room was a complication I didn't need, and I'd have to learn her story so I could figure out how to deal with her long-term. Once I dealt with the more pressing mystery, that is.

When I reached the end of my shift, Hayley walked in to take over from me, looking much more alert than she had a couple of days ago.

"What's that?" she asked Carey, peering at her laptop screen.

"Ghost research," Carey replied. "We're figuring out how to set up a ghost tour here at the inn."

"I think a karaoke night would be more popular," she said.

"Why do the coven's witches go to the Crooked Broomstick instead?" I asked. "It's much nicer here. That place looks like it's been dragged up from the bottom of the river."

"We're not part of the coven," said Hayley. "Mina won't let the coven meet at non-coven-owned locations."

I arched a brow. "It was more of a karaoke night than an actual meeting, though it'll be my last. Not just because of Marie's singing, either."

"I won't say 'I told you so'," said Carey, with a grin.

"Hey, nobody warned me there'd be singing," I said. "As well as all the arguments about shoes and broomsticks. I guess I'll have to bury all my dreams of taking up a position on the witches' council."

"They wouldn't appoint you," said Hayley, her tone uncharacteristically sharp. "They're set in their ways and only hire people who Mina personally likes."

"I know," I said. "I prefer hanging out here to dealing with coven drama. Just a joke."

The coven must be a sore point with her. Her expression softened a little as though she'd picked up on my thoughts. "Sorry. Mina and my mum didn't get along back when she was still alive."

"When did she die, in the floods?" I asked.

She shook her head. "Cancer. The coven didn't do a thing for her, so I don't feel like I owe them anything, either. I wish there was an alternative, to be honest."

"I'm sorry." I hadn't known, but it made me like Mina even less, if possible.

Allie called to me, "You can go now, Maura."

I let Hayley take over from me and went to talk to Carey's mother. "The ghost isn't causing trouble again, is she?"

"No, thankfully," she said. "I have a key to her room, so I can check up on her. You should get ready for your date with the detective."

"It's not a date," I said ineffectually. "We're going to talk to the coven healer, assuming Mina doesn't object."

"Of course." She shot me a wink over her shoulder and walked away.

Shaking my head, I went upstairs to change. At this rate, everyone except for the detective himself would be in on the shared joke.

I most definitely did not spend longer than necessary picking my outfit for that evening, without a spidery hat in sight. The ghost made no appearance in my room, thankfully, and I went down to the lobby when I was ready.

"The detective's here," said Allie, unnecessarily. I could see him through the glass doors, waiting for me.

"I'll be back later." I pushed open the door. "Hey, Drew."

He smiled at me. "Ready?"

"Sure." I fell into step alongside him as we left the inn, spotting Mart out of the corner of my eye. When I gave him a stern look, he turned his back and folded his arms. I hoped he'd get over his little huff soon, but I wouldn't deny that it was nice not to have him following me around every time the detective and I went anywhere together. "So who are we speaking to first?"

"Angie, the former coven healer," he said. "The apothecary closes in an hour, so we should go there first. As a bonus, she's no longer working for the coven, so Mina shouldn't have an issue with us speaking to her."

The apothecary sat in the main high street, nestled between a clothes shop and a bakery. We entered, and found a small room filled with barrels of herbs and containers of less savoury substances. Like floating petrified insects, for instance.

An elderly witch with piercing blue eyes behind horn-rimmed glasses sat at the wooden desk at the back of the shop, scribbling in a notebook. She glanced up as we walked in.

"Hello?" she said. "Who is it?"

"Maura," I said. "I'm new in town."

She laid down her pen. "Need a healer, do you?"

I shook my head. "No, but I heard you knew Harriet before she died, and we're looking into the possibility that her death might not have been an accident."

Angie pushed to her feet and stepped away from the desk towards a door hidden at the back of the shop. "Yes, I knew her. You'd better come in here."

She beckoned us though the door into the back room. The detective and I exchanged glances, then followed her.

The room in the back smelled so strongly of herbal concoctions that my eyes and nose began streaming almost instantly. There was nowhere to sit, so we had to awkwardly stand between piles of boxes and books and hold our arms at our sides to avoid knocking anything over. The detective in particular had to stoop under the low ceiling, while I held my breath to keep from coughing.

"So you and Harriet were close?" I managed to croak out.

"We were," she said. "Particularly in the last few weeks. She spent a fair bit of time in here, asking for my help preparing for the test."

"Test?" I said.

"For the position of coven healer," she said. "Mina had every potential healer demonstrate their skills. Harriet spent weeks preparing. She must have borrowed every book on the subject, too. If it'd been up to me, I would have given her the position for her persistence alone. She got perfect marks on the test. I saw it."

"But Mina Devlin didn't choose her," I said.

"She always has the final say." She coughed, lifting a stack of books from a chair in the corner. "This is all Harriet's work, and her preparation for the test. Do you want to take a look at the notes? There might be something useful in there."

"I'll take her notes," said the detective. "Did she come here the evening she died?"

Damn, he was sharp. I hadn't thought of that, but the former healer nodded.

"She paid me a visit early that evening," she said. "She came to me for advice on repealing the coven's decision to appoint Cathy as the healer and not her. I told her there was nothing I could do. Regardless of her performance in the examination, the council held a vote, and that was that."

"What kind of mood was she in?" asked the detective.

"It sounds like she had a rough week with the breakdown of her relationship as well."

"Oh, she took the disappointment in stride," she said. "I think she was angrier over losing out on the position of coven healer, though I don't know the details of her relationship with the werewolf. It didn't seem like a priority to her, not compared to the test."

"Whereabouts did she go after she left your shop that evening, do you know?" I asked. "Because we wondered if she might have been on her way to meet someone on the other side of the river."

"It's possible, but she didn't tell me," she said. "I was under the impression she was going home after she saw me. I closed the shop not long after and retired to bed. That was the last I saw of her." She coughed, her eyes watering.

"Did you talk about anything else?" I asked.

"Well… let me think," she said. "We discussed the coven. She made it clear she planned to leave altogether after she failed to get the position and there was clearly no repealing it. She didn't care for Mina's favouritism."

I frowned. "How long has Mina been coven leader?"

"A long time," said Angie. "I remember a time when she wasn't in charge, but I'm one of the few that does. She took over after the floods claimed the lives of some of our best witches two decades ago."

The floods again. They'd shaped the town, both in obvious ways and not-so-obvious ones. That meant Mina had led the coven for at least twenty years. A long stretch for a coven leader. Not unheard of, especially in a small community like this one, but I had an inkling something more was at work here.

"Was that when she passed the law saying there could only be one coven?" I queried.

"It's never exactly been enshrined in law, but there are too few of us to form more than one effective coven, compared to other magical communities," she said. "We have to stick together."

"Doesn't sound like that's always been the case," I said, thinking of Hayley, and what she'd said about her mother. Not to mention Harriet and how she'd been denied her dream job just because Mina had already chosen who she wanted to be the coven's healer. I didn't blame her for leaving.

But I didn't think she'd died by accident or by her own hand, either.

"Thanks for answering our questions," said Drew. "Is Cathy at work now?"

"You want to question her, do you?" asked Angie. "Yes, she's at the hospital, but be careful about disturbing her in the middle of a shift. She's under a lot of pressure, as you might imagine."

"Thanks for your help," said Drew.

The detective and I left the apothecary and walked on in silence until we came to the hospital, a tall brick building with bright flowers lining each window. Drew and I entered a waiting room full of paranormals in varying degrees of distress, and I waylaid the first nurse I saw.

"Hey," I said. "Is Cathy here?"

"She's working," she said.

"We need to talk to her," said the detective. "It's to do with an active investigation. We won't keep her for long."

"Cathy!" she bellowed. "The police are here."

Someone swore at full volume from close by, making everyone in the waiting room jump. Bemused, we followed the sound of exclamations through a door to a room where a witch sat surrounded by bubbling cauldrons. Her frizzy hair stuck out at all angles and her glasses were steamed up from the smoke billowing around her head.

"Who are you?" she asked. "Need a healer?"

"Not exactly," I said.

"Then shoo. I have patients to deal with."

Detective Drew stepped into view. "We're looking into the death of Harriet Langley. I heard you and she were rivals for the position of coven healer."

Her eyes widened. "Someone named *me* as a suspect? I was here at the hospital when she died."

That would be easy enough to verify, no doubt, but her name had come up more than once in connection to Harriet's demise. Given their supposed rivalry, I had to listen to her side of the story if I wanted to make sense of the last week's events.

Drew stepped in. "That said, we'd appreciate it if you give us a few minutes of your time."

"Fine. Ask away." She took a seat. Residue from potion ingredients stained her fingers and dark circles hung under her eyes. "We had an outbreak of a flu virus at the academy a week ago. I've been rushed off my feet ever since."

"I'm surprised you found time to take the tests to be promoted to coven healer," I remarked.

"I didn't," she said. "I couldn't even make it to my own ceremony and took the healer's test from here at the hospital. Mina wasn't pleased, but I can't be in two places at once."

"Have you seen Angie lately, then?" I asked. "I gathered Harriet spent a lot of time with her."

"Of course she did," she said. "Harriet saved up all her leave so she could take most of the last couple of weeks off to study for the test. Some of us had to stay at work."

"Then when did you hear about her death?"

"The next day." She yawned. "Anyway, I'd ask Harriet to back me up, but I don't know whereabouts she went."

"What?" I frowned. "You don't mean her ghost?"

"I thought you knew," she said. "You can see them, right? Not many witches in the coven can, but she knew *I* could, so she came straight here after her death to tell me I shouldn't have got the job. It's downright distracting to have a ghost telling you off, I can tell you that much."

Well. That changes things. "Believe me, I get that. Is she still here?"

"How would I know?" she said. "I've been on night shifts all week and sleeping during the day. I haven't been watching out for ghosts. All she did was follow me around telling me I'm inadequate."

"That's all?" said Drew.

"Yeah, she was relentless," she said. "At first she didn't seem to know she was dead. Then she went into a kind of existential crisis and wandered off somewhere to reflect on life and death."

"Really?" I asked. "She didn't say anything about how she died. Didn't you ask her?"

"It was more of a one-sided conversation," she said. "I'm not sure she could even hear me. Anyway, she took off and I haven't seen her since."

"Do you know where she might have gone?" I asked. "Because so far, I haven't seen any signs of her."

She shrugged. "I thought she was going to haunt me for weeks. I won't complain if she doesn't, but it wouldn't surprise me if someone banished her to get her off their hands."

"Banished her?" Only people who could actually see ghosts would stand a chance of banishing her, not if they didn't know where she was hiding. "Like who?"

"Like her ex's new partner, for instance," she said. "I assumed she went to haunt them both after she finished haunting me."

"Lisa can see ghosts?" I asked.

"Sure," she said. "I thought Harriet went to terrorise her. Or Mina, but she can't see ghosts herself, so there wouldn't be much point."

Huh. I hadn't asked Lisa if she could see ghosts, but maybe I should have done. Both she and Maxwell would have good reason to want to get rid of Harriet's roaming spirit.

"Thanks for speaking to us," said the detective. "I'll let you know if I need anything else from you."

The two of us left the hospital, while Cathy returned to stirring potions and swearing under her breath.

"What do you think?" asked Drew. "It does sound like Cathy was telling the truth. She certainly had a solid alibi for the time of Harriet's death. We can confirm with any of the other staff here."

"Yeah, but if Harriet's ghost was around, you'd think she'd have checked on her ex," I said. "Or at least gone home to stop him from stealing any of her stuff. That's what I'd have done."

He arched a brow. "Oh? Anyone in particular you'd want to haunt?"

"None of my exes are worth the attention, but I'd rather choose who gets to keep my stuff after I die." Too late, I remembered who I was talking to, and felt a flush creep up my face. "I'm not planning on dying anytime soon, besides. I think it's worth checking with Lisa to see if Cathy's claim holds up."

Unless Cathy had been less than truthful, that is, but I didn't see why she'd have reason to lie about being visited by Harriet's ghost. She clearly had a lot going on.

"I think we should talk to Maxwell again, too," he said. "He might not be able to see her ghost, but if we tell him that Cathy did, it might be a way to gauge his reaction to her sticking around after her death."

"Good thinking." I slowed my pace, noting that we were closer to Harriet's old house than Maxwell and Lisa's place. "If Harriet's ghost ran off recently, she might have gone back home after all. I think we should check the house again."

He nodded. "All right. I still have the key."

We walked the short distance to Harriet's house, where the detective unlocked the front door. Someone had removed most of the plants from the windowsills, perhaps her family, though her house still held a somewhat lived-in look despite the boxes scattered around the hallway.

"Has her family been here?" I asked.

"They have," he said. "The notes from Angie's shop will be more useful as evidence than anything here, I think, given how much of the last few weeks she spent there."

I went upstairs first. No signs of any hiding ex-boyfriends this time around—nor any ghosts, either. I paced around the room, then closed my eyes, as though it would help me to access my Reaper senses.

"What are you doing?" asked Drew.

"Seeing if I can sense her ghost using my Reaper skills." I opened my eyes. "Can't sense her in here, though."

"Is there another way for you to track a specific ghost?" he asked.

I should have expected that question... and it was starting to seem like the only remaining option. "It's doable, but I haven't tried doing that for years. If I want to pull it off, I need something of hers. Something important to her. Like I could work with a childhood toy, or something she had strong emotions attached to."

"Will this do?" Drew held up a rumpled photo of her and Maxwell. That would have strong feelings attached to it, I had no doubt.

"That works." I took it from him and held it up, and let shadows unfold around me, my attention focused on the photo.

A faint gasp from Drew made me lower my gaze. Oops. I'd accidentally flooded the whole room with shadows, pulling the detective with me halfway into the afterlife.

"What are you doing?" Drew's eyes widened, taking in the sight of the blanket of shadows which had replaced the floor.

"Ah." Flustered, I tried to pull the shadows back, and a sudden tugging sensation gripped the photo in my hand. "This is just the afterworld. Nothing can harm you here."

"I'll take your word for it." A hint of a growl filled his voice, but I was too focused on the photo to figure out how to deal with that. The tugging sensation pulled me towards... a door.

Damn. My Reaper senses had hit a dead end. She wasn't here. In Hawkwood Hollow... or anywhere else. Not in the land of the living, anyway.

I let the shadows fold outwards until the house returned to normal. Drew met my eyes. "That was..."

"An accident," I said. "Sorry. I don't make a habit of yanking living people with me into the afterlife." In fact, the only other time I'd done it had been when Carey and I had been stuck in Mrs Renner's house, and I'd been forced to use the shadows to stop us from falling through the floor when the house collapsed.

"I gathered," he said. "What did you see?"

He was taking this pretty well. I knew the afterlife was terrifying to outsiders—and some Reapers, come to that—but he still seemed composed. Didn't make me less inclined to feel like I ought to hop over to the other side for a bit and hide out of sheer embarrassment.

"Nothing," I said. "She's gone."

"How?" he asked. "Was she banished by another Reaper?"

"Unlikely," I said. "It's possible she moved on by herself. Not likely, considering how ghost-friendly this town is, but the only other possibility is that someone else in town banished her ghost on purpose."

"Why?" he asked. "Because they wanted to ensure she didn't talk?"

"Precisely my thinking," I said. "I've yet to find anyone aside from Cathy in the coven who can actually see ghosts. Oh... and Lisa. But she's not part of the coven."

Who was the more likely culprit of the pair of them?

We'd already questioned Cathy thoroughly, but perhaps Lisa had felt threatened by Harriet's ghost's presence in her new life. Or maybe neither of them had done it.

Whoever was responsible, banishing a spirit in a town like this didn't strike me as a decision taken lightly. Either the culprit didn't want her to haunt them—or they didn't want the truth to get out about Harriet's death.

In other words, they didn't want the ghost to come to me.

It was a stretch, I admitted, but I'd acquired something of a reputation since the incident with Mrs Renner and it seemed like the whole coven knew I was half-Reaper. Judging by the snide comments I'd faced at the coven meeting, I assumed that was the case, anyway.

Regardless, someone had banished Harriet's ghost. Someone who didn't want a Reaper getting involved in the investigation, perhaps. That might be paranoid of me, but so few people could even see or speak to ghosts that it was hard for me to discount the possibility.

It might not be personal… but I couldn't afford to take that chance.

I turned to Drew. "I think we should have a word with the coven leader again. I wonder what she'll have to say about the ghost's disappearance?"

8

———————————

The universe had other plans, however. Firstly, Mina Devlin didn't answer when I knocked on her office door. A new sign affixed to the wooden surface said her office hours were between ten and four, which hadn't been there the last time we'd been here. Now that was a rebuff if I ever saw one.

"What's the betting she put that thing up just to get rid of me?" I remarked.

"That's not professional of her, if it's true," said Drew.

"She's coven leader, so she gets to do whatever she likes," I said. "I guess asking her who might have banished Harriet's ghost is off the table, unless we go to her home address."

No chance. She'd probably hex us into oblivion if we disturbed her at home.

The detective paused for an instant. "Would the Reaper be able to tell who banished her? He might have seen her ghost himself."

I frowned. "I guess it's worth asking, but if it was a

magical banishment with no need for a Reaper, he probably wasn't paying any attention."

Still... he had a point. The retired Reaper must know about Harriet's death. Maybe he knew where her ghost had gone, too. The guy might not want to do his job, but that didn't change the fact that the dead gathered wherever he went. We had that much in common.

The detective and I walked towards the town's cemetery. The Reaper lived in a cottage at the foot of the hill, bizarrely numbered 42 for reasons I hadn't yet figured out. What he'd been doing with his time since his retirement twenty years earlier, I hadn't a clue. At least the detective was with me, which made him less likely to slam the door in my face.

"What?" growled the Reaper's voice when I knocked.

"It's Maura," I said. "I wanted to ask you a question. About a ghost."

The door didn't open. "If you want me to get rid of that brother of yours, do it yourself."

"That's not what this is about," I said indignantly. "Detective Drew is with me. We're looking into a recent case of a witch who died in suspicious circumstances, and we believe someone banished her ghost to stop us from getting to the truth."

"I don't banish ghosts anymore," he growled. "I'm retired."

"I'm not accusing you of doing the banishing, but I'd appreciate your help so I can figure out who did."

The door wrenched open and Harold the Reaper appeared, affording me a view of his dingy cottage. Including his scythe, leaning against the wall, from which he'd hung a dozen cloaks. Guess that answered the question of whether my arrival in town had inspired him to take up Reaping again. His grey hair hung around his face, while his face was twisted in a perpetual scowl. Right now, it was directed at Drew as much as it was me.

"You've managed to solve all your homicide cases until now without getting me involved, Detective," he said. "I'm sure you can handle this one, too."

I stepped in. "Look, we just wanted to ask if you've seen Harriet's ghost."

"She drowned in the river earlier this week," said Drew. "I believed her death was an accident, but we recently learned that her ghost was seen haunting a rival of hers. The ghost has since vanished."

"When I tried using my abilities to track her ghost, she was gone," I added. "I doubt she moved on by herself."

"Really?" he said. "Maybe your Reaper abilities need some fine-tuning."

I matched his scowl with one of my own. "Trust me, I'd know if she was still around, and she isn't. All I wanted to know is if you can confirm whether she moved on. Or not."

He grunted. "I don't keep an eye on that kind of thing anymore. If your own Reaper senses told you she's not here, she moved on, and that's that."

"Is there a way for me to figure out who banished her, though?" I said. "Would they have to be able to see her in order to do it?"

"You already know the answer to that, unless you're less of a witch than you say you are." He retreated into the hallway and shut the door in my face.

I turned to Drew with a sigh. "Guess it couldn't have a simple answer, huh."

"It's still more likely someone who could see her ghost was responsible for getting rid of her," he said. "If nothing else, they'd be able to verify her location before they did it."

Smart of him. Considering he'd never dealt with ghosts before I'd arrived in town, he'd caught on pretty well to how the whole thing worked. "You're right, but I wish I knew where to go from here."

"For now, home," he said. "My colleagues are waiting for an explanation as to why I'm focusing all my attention on this case, so I have to give one to them."

"Tell them to go and hassle the coven leader," I said. "Mina can't hide from me forever. I'm sure she must know more than she let on. She wouldn't have barred me from her office if she didn't. Unless I really annoyed her that much. Which is possible. I get told I'm annoying a lot."

"If it helps, I find you perfectly charming."

A flush swept my cheeks. "I'm pretty sure nobody has ever called me charming before."

"I'm surprised."

My heart kick-started. "Um, you do remember I dragged you into the afterlife, right?"

"Yes, I do."

Ack. Why did I have to remind him? I clamped my mouth shut before I made an even bigger fool of myself. "I'll see you later."

We parted ways, and I walked back over the bridge towards the inn. I kept both eyes open for ghosts, though by now, I was convinced Harriet was long gone. Someone had seen to that. Someone who would be getting a stern talking-to from me… once I figured out who it was, anyway. With luck, I'd do a better job of that than I had of taking a compliment from the detective.

A sudden chilling wail echoed from the direction of the inn as I approached. *Oh, no. What now?*

It seemed the ghost was having another bad day. I walked through the glass doors to the lobby, where several people milled about, looking at the ceiling and muttering among themselves. Howling echoed from upstairs, and when I entered the restaurant, I found Carey's mother helping Hayley deal cast soundproofing spells all over the walls.

"The ghost is at it again," said Allie.

"What set her off this time?" I winced as a particularly loud screech rattled the cutlery and glasses on the tables.

"No idea," she said. "I tried opening the door to her room, but I couldn't hear a word she said, and she wouldn't listen to me. She just kept on screaming."

"Ah, sorry," I said. "I'll see what the problem is."

I ran for the stairs, cursing the ghost for ensuring I never got a moment to relax. If it turned out Mart had been the one who'd set her off, I wouldn't be amused in the slightest. If only Harriet had been the ghost who'd showed up in my room instead. That would have saved me a great deal of trouble, I'd say that much.

Mart greeted me at the top of the stairs. "Help me! I'm being deafened."

"What's the problem?" I walked past him and towards the room next to mine. It was already unlocked, since Allie had already tried to calm the ghost down and failed.

Inside the room, the ghost floated in mid-air and howled at the ceiling. She had an impressive set of lungs on her for someone who, well, didn't have lungs. She must be projecting her voice all the way around the hotel, which came as a surprise considering she'd hardly been able to speak at all the last time we'd seen one another. Now every person inside the inn *and* the restaurant would know she was here.

"Hey!" I said. "Mandy, calm down."

She momentarily quietened down long enough to give me a reproachful look. "You were gone."

"You were calling for me?" I asked.

"Yes," she said.

"What is it you wanted to say?" I closed the door behind me. "I'm kind of busy. Unless… do you remember anything else about how you died?"

"I remembered my full name," she announced. "It's Amanda Dawson."

The name didn't ring a bell, but it wasn't like I knew everyone who'd ever died here in Hawkwood Hollow. Ghosts were all different and some of them never recalled their former lives before their deaths. Others drifted around in a happy delusion until they finally moved on. Mandy, on the other hand, must have been around a while, though I'd need to get confirmation to find out just how long. Maybe I could ask about her now I knew her full name. In all the free time I didn't have.

"Okay," I said. "Is there a reason you picked out my room to haunt?"

"You're safe," she said. "You won't let them banish me."

I blinked at her. "By 'them', who do you mean?"

She shook her head. "I don't remember."

She can't mean the coven, can she? The witches were on my mind because of the disappearance of Harriet's ghost, but suspicion gripped me all the same. Hadn't she shown up here the same night Harriet had died?

"Will you please try to keep the noise down next time?" I asked. "The whole inn could hear you. If you were trying to avoid attention, there are better ways of going about it."

She shrank back. "I didn't know they could hear. Oh, no. Oh, no."

"Mart will watch you," I reassured her. "We won't let anyone banish you. Look, if you just stay put and keep quiet, you'll be fine."

"They're coming for me!" she whimpered.

"There's a dozen other ghosts in the building and countless more outside of it," I told her. "Nobody's looking for you, and no one will find you."

I wasn't sure she heard me, but I closed the door behind me. Footsteps on the stairs alerted me to Allie's arrival.

"Is the ghost okay?" she asked.

"For now," I said. "She kind of had a meltdown because she remembered her full name and thinks someone's coming here to banish her. Now she knows everyone can hear her, she'll be quiet."

"Really?" Interest gleamed in her eyes. "Who is she?"

"Do you know of a witch called Amanda Dawson?" I asked Allie.

"Amanda..." She paused. "Yes, a witch in the coven who died a few years back."

"She was in the coven?" I frowned. "So she's been dead a while. I wonder what prompted her to come back here."

Was it a coincidence that she'd shown up in my room so soon after Harriet's death? Her memory might take more prompting to turn up anything useful, but that didn't make it impossible to find out the truth. I had a detective on my side for a reason.

"I couldn't say," said Allie. "Maybe ask the coven leader?"

I made a sceptical noise. "She stuck a note on her door with a made-up set of office hours just to get rid of me. I doubt she'll be amused if I start bombarding her for details of a witch who died years ago. I also don't think she can see ghosts herself, so she might just dismiss me as a troublemaker."

"I'm sure if the detective is with you, she won't say no," she said.

I decided not to argue. I'd had quite enough conflict for one day, and I didn't want to backtrack when I'd made more progress with the ghost than I ever thought I would. I knew her name now, and with that information, maybe the detective would be able to find records of her death. If he had time to, what with the ongoing issue of Harriet's ghost's disappearance.

"I'd better tell the guests that you've dealt with the trouble," she added. "Thanks for handling her, Maura."

Maybe that should be my official title. Ghost-handler. It wasn't like I'd do a worse job at that than I had at ingratiating myself with the coven.

I returned to my room and picked up my phone to send a message to Drew. As I hit send, Mart floated through the wall, his arms folded across his chest. "You're letting her stay after she deafened everyone in the building?"

"For now." I kept my voice low. "Don't provoke her.

She used to be part of the coven... aka, the same coven who might have been involved in Harriet's death."

"If anything, that's a good reason *not* to let her stay," he said. "She thinks someone is going to banish her. What if they banish me, too?"

"Mart, I can't be in five places at once," I said. "Nobody is going to banish you."

He scoffed. "I'm being replaced by another ghost."

"Don't be absurd." I really didn't have time for his arguments. "How would you feel if you were a terrified ghost and another spirit kept hassling you?"

"I'm going to sleep outside." He pointedly turned away.

"You don't sleep," I said as he floated through the door.

This was going to end well.

───

The following morning, I woke with a new plan. Seeing the coven leader was top of my list, but I also needed to figure out how to deal with the ghost. Now everyone could hear her, she had the potential to make life very difficult for me. Almost as difficult as my brother, who still wasn't speaking to me. When I saw Mart downstairs, he stuck his nose in the air and floated right past me as though I didn't exist. Luckily, Drew texted me saying he was on his way and met me in the lobby after breakfast.

"What's going on?" he asked. "I heard something about a disturbance here yesterday."

"The ghost," I said. "She remembered her name, and she also remembered how to throw a tantrum so that the entire inn could hear. I managed to calm her down, but now my brother's sulking because I won't get rid of her. It's all ghost drama over here."

"I got your message earlier," he said. "Do you still want to speak to Mina? We're within her opening hours, so she can't say she's too busy to see us. Maybe she can tell us who might have banished Harriet's ghost."

"Not sure if she'll be much help," I said. "If a witch performed the banishing spell, they'd have needed to use certain herbs for it to work. We could visit Angie again. She's bound to remember if anyone bought the right herbs for a banishment. That might point us in the right direction."

"Some witches grow their own herbs, don't they?" said Drew. "Not dismissing your idea, mind."

"Yes, but it's still worth checking out," I said. "Maybe Angie remembers something she didn't tell us last time, too. Also, I have a new line of questioning."

"Oh?" he said. "Is that the new information you mentioned in your message?"

"I found out the ghost in my room used to be part of the local coven, too," I explained. "She remembered her name. Amanda Dawson. She died a while ago, but for some reason, her ghost showed up the same night Harriet died. Seems fishy to me."

He frowned. "I can check for the details, but my colleagues are starting to question if I'm operating on a hunch and not concrete evidence already."

"More of a Reaper sense than a hunch." To people who weren't Reapers, though, there wasn't much of a difference. I didn't blame the others for being sceptical.

But I knew there was something significant in the

appearance of Amanda's ghost. Something that linked to the coven, past and present.

"Hunch or not, I trust your word," he said.

The rush of warm pride that flooded me almost made the whole thing worth it. I suppressed a grin. "I'm cracking under the pressure."

"I'm sure you'll survive it."

We walked along the same route as yesterday, towards the high street. Not many people were around, while the apothecary itself was dark behind the windows despite being within opening hours. Strange.

I knocked. Then the detective pushed the door inwards.

At once, I knew something was wrong. The place held an air of abandonment, even though it hadn't been long since we'd last been here. But the shadows folding around the edges were hard to ignore, and I was already prepared when my Reaper senses kicked in, too late, telling me there was nobody living in here aside from the two of us. The body that lay sprawled behind the counter confirmed my worst fears.

The healer was dead.

9

"Poisoned," said Mina Devlin. "By a concoction of herbs someone slipped inside her teacup."

"Who would have done that?" whispered Fran.

The other witches crowded into the small shop. They'd come here with their leader as soon as Drew had sent for her, and their shocked murmurs filled the air along with the scent of herbs.

It was lucky the chief of police had been the one to discover her body, or else I might have ended up in a world of trouble, given the accusing looks some of the witches shot in my direction. I could just hear the rumours about the newbie who'd shown up to their coven meeting suddenly discovering the dead body of a beloved retired coven member not long after. They didn't bother to hide their disdain for my presence here, but I didn't want to leave without something resembling an answer.

Especially as this time, my Reaper senses hadn't reacted to her death at all.

"How long has she been in here?" I asked.

"Overnight, I'd guess," said Marie. "Didn't you come and visit yesterday?"

All eyes turned to me.

"Both of us did," the detective interjected. "As part of my ongoing investigation into Harriet's death. We left the shop together, and Maura hasn't been back here since then."

Uneasiness rippled through the group, and to my intense relief, their attention withdrew from me for a bit as they whispered among themselves. One of the witches waved a wand over Angie's body, muttering under her breath. Forensic magic wasn't my forte, but I gathered she was discerning more information about the cause of death. Not summoning her ghost... though that didn't require a spell. It would likely take another day or so for her spirit to show up, and while I wanted to have another look around the shop, the coven leader continued to glare at me in a manner I found vaguely insulting. Did she really think I'd murder a harmless old woman?

Getting my Reaper powers out to see if I could track her ghost was out of the question, because the witches would probably hex me on the spot. Though with the detective on my side, the odds of ending up jailed were comfortably low enough for me to risk staying here while they conducted their spells.

The witch waving her wand lowered her hand, her mouth pursed. "She was definitely poisoned. About ten hours or so ago, give or take."

Then she'd been lying here all night. A chill raced down my back. Her killer had been here only a few hours after our visit and had been content to leave her here, undiscovered. Yet for all that, my Reaper senses had chosen to remain dormant.

"Poisoned by what?" asked Marie.

"This." Mina indicated a cup. "Someone concocted a lethal dose of a rare and deadly poison, no doubt from her own supplies."

My gaze drifted across the shelves. The ingredients here in the shop might create a dozen varieties of poison, and the floating insects in jars appeared even more disturbing than before.

While the apothecary wouldn't be the only place the ingredients might have come from, how many people among the witches had the necessary knowledge to concoct a rare poison? Cathy, as the new healer, must have in-depth knowledge, so maybe *she'd* been the one to come here to poison her predecessor. But that made little sense either, given that she already had the job she wanted.

The only other place I'd seen a large number of rare herbs had been Harriet's house, but again, she was already dead. Still, we definitely needed another word with the ex-boyfriend.

As the witches broke into yet another argument, the detective beckoned me aside. "I doubt I'll get away from this one for a while. It's definitely a case of premediated murder."

"I don't expect you to," I whispered back. "I don't think there's anything I can do here, either."

"I have to stay," said Drew in apologetic tones. "This needs to be sorted out. I'd advise you to leave, before…"

"Before Mina kicks me out," I finished. "Yeah, I figured. Text me when you're done here, okay?"

The coven leader would definitely not be in the mood to answer my questions about the ghost of a dead coven member in my room at the inn, that was for certain. I'd have to wait until the madness had calmed down before I brought up the subject with her.

Instead, I headed back to the inn, trying to quell the suspicion that my own visit to Angie's shop had sparked her death. I couldn't be the only person who'd heard that Angie had been the last person to see Harriet alive, surely, but racking my brains didn't turn up another explanation. One way or another, I'd screwed up. Majorly.

Allie waved at me from behind the desk in the lobby. "Hey, Maura. Did something else happen?"

"Angie was murdered," I said. "Poisoned in her own shop."

She clapped her hands to her mouth. "Who'd have done such a thing?"

"Someone who might have realised she'd spoken to Harriet just before her death," I said. "I was the one who went there to ask her if she'd seen Harriet. If I hadn't…"

"It's not your fault," she said. "You couldn't possibly have guessed this might happen."

I couldn't help feeling that it was, but the person responsible must know that they couldn't keep that information under wraps forever. But why would they kill her? Because they thought Angie might have guessed the person responsible for Harriet's death? If she had, she sure hadn't told me, anyway. Or might they have killed her because they knew the detective and I were going back there today? Questions rioted in my mind with no answers forthcoming.

In the meantime, I went to talk to the ghost at the inn again. Mandy ducked out of sight when I walked into her room, as though expecting me to start yelling at her.

"Hey," I said to her. "I'm not going to hurt you."

She didn't answer. Who was she hiding from? The coven, or whoever had been responsible for her death? I didn't want to push her and end up back at square one, but now a second person had shown up dead. I really needed to know if Mandy's own death was linked to recent events, if just for my own peace of mind. With Mina Devlin even less likely to cooperate with me now, I had few options available.

"Did you know Angie?" I asked, figuring I might as well start with that.

"She's the coven's healer," she said.

"She was," I said. "She retired last week. Then someone murdered her today."

"Murdered!" Her eyes flew wide. "Why?"

I sat down on the bed. "It's the same person who killed Harriet, I think. Angie was the last person to see her alive, so I think someone wanted to ensure she didn't figure out who the killer was."

She sank into a sitting position. "Please don't tell anyone I'm here."

"I won't," I said, keeping my tone gentle. "Do you remember how you died yet?"

She froze. "No. No, no, no."

"Okay, you don't have to push yourself if you don't want to." But what if she *did* know something which might lead to the truth? If Mandy was afraid someone would come after her, then her concerns might be legitimate. The last person we'd questioned was dead. That was an indisputable fact. Something had driven her here, and her fear of being banished was genuine.

And I'd protect her until she was ready to share the truth.

———

I left the ghost in her room and helped Allie with various tasks around the inn while I waited to hear from Drew.

Mart, of course, was nowhere to be seen. I'd have gone looking for him, but at the rate at which I was wrecking things lately, I'd only end up furthering his grudge against our ghostly neighbour if I tried confronting him now.

Drew finally came back to the inn around mid-afternoon, and I met him in the lobby.

"Hey," I said to the detective. "Safely escaped Mina's clutches in one piece, did you?"

"Just about," he replied. "She insisted on taking all the books Angie gave me from the back room of the apothecary. The books Harriet was studying before her death."

"Seriously?" I swore. "She can't do that. Aren't those evidence?"

"My colleagues finished looking through them and concluded there wasn't anything in the books worth keeping them for," he said. "They also agreed to hand the bulk of the investigating over to Mina Devlin after she marched into the office and yelled at everyone."

"Of course she did," I said. "Next you'll be telling me she asked you to arrest me as a suspect."

"She didn't, but she told me to inform you to forget about ever joining the coven," he said.

"I'm devastated." I gave an eye-roll. "I got out my best hat for nothing."

"If it helps, I've officially struck you off the suspect list," he added. "My colleagues want me to prioritise this case over Harriet's death, but we can do both, as long as we don't tread on Mina's toes."

"I'd like to walk over her feet with a pair of heavy boots,' I said. "Whereabouts are we supposed to go that won't end up with us conflicting with her? She pretty much owns the entirety of the witches' area of town."

"I doubt she's considered speaking to Maxwell and Lisa," he said. "Maxwell isn't a witch, and Lisa has never been part of the coven. I checked."

"Good enough," I said. "Not sure if she and Angie knew one another, but they must at least have been aware that Angie was the coven healer and that Harriet wanted to be her successor."

Neither of them struck me as likely to have killed the old healer, but I'd have liked to talk to Lisa about her ability to see ghosts, and it would be a good way to pass the time before Angie's ghost showed up. *If* she showed up, then I'd need to make sure I got there before whoever had banished the last one did the same again.

Drew and I reached Maxwell and Lisa's house, and the detective rang the doorbell. Lisa answered, her hair heaped on her head in a bun, looking surprised to see us.

"Is Maxwell in?" asked the Detective.

"No," she said. "He's at work."

"Okay, then can we speak to you alone?" I asked.

"Sure." She didn't sound happy, but she let us into the

house. "I thought I'd already answered all your questions, detective."

"Did you hear the retired healer died yesterday?" I asked.

"Angie?" Her eyes widened. "No. I didn't."

Guess the coven didn't tell the town's non-members. "I'm told you can see ghosts."

"Who said that?" she said. "What does it matter?"

"It matters because Harriet's ghost was banished," I said. "Did you see her?"

"Is that what this is about?" she asked. "I didn't see her ghost. I didn't even know she *was* one."

"Have you always been able to see ghosts?" asked Drew.

"Yes, but they're mostly background noise," she said. "It'd be weird *not* to see them. I swear I didn't see Harriet, though."

I knew I was supposed to be asking about Angie, but I couldn't help wondering what it would have been like to grow up in a place like this when you could see ghosts. While my own childhood had been unconventional even in the magical world, at least I'd known from the start that I was half-Reaper and I'd been given the tools to handle it. Given the coven leader's attitude, I doubted she'd have bothered trying to help her fellow witches who had the misfortune to be able to see Hawkwood Hollow's extra residents. They'd have just had to put up with being haunted wherever they went.

On the other hand, why would Harriet have gone to haunt Cathy and not come here? Maybe she was angrier about losing out on the coven healer position than she was about her breakup, but if Lisa or Cathy hadn't banished her, who had?

"When did the two of you meet?" I asked. "You and Maxwell?"

"Oh, about six months ago," she said. "He works in the bookshop, and I fell for him right away."

I tilted my head. "I thought the two of you only got together last week."

"Officially," said Drew. "Were you seeing each other before then?"

She fidgeted. "Um. Max didn't want Harriet to know, but…"

"But she's dead," I finished. "So you can tell us the truth now."

"We met up a few times, but I knew there was something real from the start," she said. "He always wanted to be with me. He was just too nice to finish things with Harriet."

"I wouldn't call it nice, if he cheated on her," I said. "How long were you seeing each other before he told her?"

"Six weeks."

I winced inwardly. I'd bet Harriet had known. That sort of thing was difficult to hide. It might explain why she hadn't come back here to haunt them. She'd been resigned to losing Maxwell already, and it might even have been a relief when he'd finally moved out.

On the other hand, I'd have to speak to Maxwell himself if I wanted to hear his side of the story.

The detective and I left the house after asking for directions to the bookshop where Maxwell worked.

"I think that's progress," I said. "I don't think she's the one who banished Harriet's ghost, anyway."

"You think she was telling the truth?" Drew said.

"I actually do," I said. "I don't think Harriet was all that surprised to find out about Maxwell's cheating. I bet she was relieved to have him gone."

"Then we'll see if he backs up Lisa's story," he said.

D rew and I entered the local bookshop, where we found the werewolf standing on a ladder to return some books to a high shelf. The blond muscular man appeared out of place in the cosy shop next to the piles of old books, and when we entered, he hopped off the ladder. "You again?"

"That's us," I said. "We just wanted to ask you a few more questions."

"Ask away." His gaze darted towards the door, as though he hoped someone would show up and rescue him.

Drew stepped in first. "You might be aware that the coven's retired healer was found dead in her shop yesterday. Murdered."

"What?" he yelped. "I'm a werewolf. We don't hire healers from the coven. I've never been to her shop in my life."

"We have reason to believe her murder was linked with Harriet's death, so I felt it necessary to question the same suspects again," said the detective. "We already spoke to Lisa, and while we don't believe she murdered the healer, some questions about your relationship came up."

"Like what?" His eyes darted between us, his expression bemused. "Lisa wasn't involved either."

I drew in a breath. "Lisa told us that you and she already had a relationship going when you were still living with Harriet."

A flush rose on his cheeks. "She told you that?"

"Yeah," I said. "Did Harriet know?"

"I think she suspected," he muttered. "It was hard to hide anything from her even with her working long hours and studying all the time. It was a relief to get it all out in the open."

"And you're sure Harriet was fine with it all?"

He shrugged. "I dunno. She wasn't happy for a while, but she wanted the position of coven healer and she was focused on that. Not on our relationship."

That fit with what Lisa had said, and it would explain why her ghost hadn't come to their house. Not when she'd already been resigned to breaking up with him and she'd been focused on the position of coven healer... which she'd lost out on anyway.

But I still felt like I was missing something. Where did Mandy's ghost's appearance fit into it all? It wasn't any use asking Maxwell about her, since as a werewolf, he wouldn't know the identities of every coven member who'd died in town over the last few years. Besides, after Angie's death, I needed to be careful what I said, and to whom.

The detective's phone buzzed in his pocket. "I'll come back if I have more questions. Thank you for your time."

I ducked out of the shop after him as he took the call and waited for him to finish speaking on the phone. From his tone, it sounded like the police were on the other end, probably checking up on him.

"I have to head back to the office," he said. "If I can get permission to go and speak to Cathy at the hospital again, it's an option, but I'm inclined to believe Lisa and Maxwell aren't involved."

"Me too," I said, "but I feel like we're missing something somewhere. Who else might have known her ghost was around and decided to banish her?"

I was also starting to suspect that Harriet's relationship drama had taken a back seat when it came to the events which had led to her death. No, the truth likely lay with the coven, which made it all the more frustrating that they'd been utterly unwelcoming to me. Witches were the only paranormals who had the ability to see ghosts—aside from Reapers, of course. And it sounded like all the witches she'd been close to in life had been part of the coven.

With Mina Devlin overlooking everything, I needed to be sneakier if I wanted answers. In the meantime, I was determined to find the healer's ghost before whoever had banished Harriet got to her, too.

———

I waited for sunset before slipping out of the inn and heading across the bridge back to the witches' part of town. Then I made for Angie's shop, hoping I hadn't made a mistake in leaving Drew out of this. After I'd accidentally dragged him into Death, I'd rather avoid getting him involved in any ghost-hunting shenanigans. Especially ones Mina Devlin would disapprove of.

I trod through the darkness to the shop. The place was deserted, as expected, though the petrified insects floating in jars were freakier than any ghost. As I walked, I cast a quick warmth spell to make myself less like I'd walked into a giant freezer. The old healer had lived in the flat above the main shop, so there was no more likely place for her ghost to show up than in here.

It looked like Mina had stripped the place of anything which might count as potential evidence, but I still had a quick poke around the shelves in search of any samples of ghost-banishing herbs. It took several minutes of stumbling around in the dark between shelves until I had all the bottles stashed in my pockets. Removing them from the shop probably wouldn't deter anyone who really wanted rid of her, but I could at least delay them a little.

Then I stood at the back and waited for the ghost to show up. Spirits were more likely to appear at night, and it'd already been more than twenty-four hours since her death. *Come on, Angie...*

In the darkness, the door creaked, and there came the faint sound of footsteps. I held my breath. That wasn't a ghost. Someone had come into the shop. Someone very much alive... and breaking and entering.

I crept forward, wand in hand, and peered at the tall figure creeping through the shadows.

You've got to be kidding me.

Mina Devlin glared at me. "You. I knew you were up to no good."

"Speak for yourself." I pressed a hand to my thumping heart. "What are you doing in here?"

"It's my business," she said. "What are *you* doing?"

"I'm part of an official police investigation," I told her.

"I think we both know there is nothing official about this," she said. "Thought you'd steal from Angie's private stores, did you?"

She wasn't wrong, though not for the reasons she assumed. "I came here to speak to Angie's ghost."

"I don't see any spirits," she said.

"Thought you couldn't see them anyway." I bit down another less savoury remark. "I know it takes roughly a day for a ghost to appear, and given that Harriet's ghost vanished before I could speak to her, I wanted to be sure I got here in time to speak to Angie."

"Vanished?" Her eyes narrowed. "Who told you that?"

Tread carefully. "I spoke to Cathy, who saw Harriet's ghost shortly after her death. But she hasn't been seen since, and considering the high number of ghosts in town, I figured it couldn't be accidental. I was going to speak to you about it earlier, but when the detective and I found Angie's body here, we had to put that plan on hold."

"So you admit to your involvement in her death?" she said.

"I think there's a good chance the person who killed her did so to stop Drew and me from finding out the truth about who killed Harriet." I knew I was digging myself a bigger hole, but I couldn't bring myself to give a crap. "If you agree, the police would appreciate your help."

"Don't try that with me," she said. "I know you're involving yourself in this out of your own curiosity, not because you were invited to assist the chief of police."

I held her gaze. "I work with ghosts. It's hard not to get involved in cases where they disappear when they shouldn't."

"Who are you to say they shouldn't?" she said. "You're not the Reaper. You claimed to aspire to join my coven, and yet you're here breaking into the home of one of our valued members."

"You weren't exactly welcoming to me," I told her. "I might not want to join the coven, but that doesn't mean I don't care about the deaths of two of its members."

She strode up to me until we stood nose to nose. "If you value your safety, I would. The coven's business is ours alone, not yours, and not the police's."

"I could ask what *you're* doing here," I said, a surge of recklessness rising within me. "You're breaking and entering, too."

The coven leader scoffed. "This shop is now the property of the coven. You're trespassing. Leave, *now.*"

Her sharp tone hit me like a whip, but I held her gaze. "If I find out her ghost has been banished..."

"You'll do what?" she said. "I wouldn't pick a fight with the coven, Maura. Reaper or not, you'll lose."

And everyone in the coven is cool with you breaking onto the property of your former healer? At least I'd swiped the herbs for a banishment spell. That ought to delay her a little if she planned to act against the ghost.

"Nobody said anything about fighting," I said. "Good luck with whatever you're doing here in the middle of the night."

And with that, I turned around and left the shop. *That went almost as well as my attempt to join the coven.* Doubtless the detective would not be thrilled to learn what I'd done, but I'd had to try, for Angie's sake if nobody else's.

On impulse, I cloaked myself in shadows and came to a halt outside the shop, waiting for her to leave. Minutes trickled by, and the cold bit through my clothes. I risked another peek into the shop, but my Reaper senses were as dormant as the sensation in my feet.

No ghost showed up. When Mina approached the door, empty-handed, I headed back to the inn, hoping I hadn't made a huge mistake. It wasn't like I'd had a chance in hell of joining the coven anyway, and Mina was a prime example of the kind of authority figure I'd always struggled not to come into conflict with. Leading the coven didn't give her licence to act like she ruled the entire town.

If I'd done a better job of convincing her I'd wanted to join the coven from the start, I might not be in this mess, but she'd been set against me before we'd even met face to face, and I'd only end up in worse trouble if I confronted her now.

Breaking into Angie's shop didn't necessarily indicate guilt, but if she *did* turn out to be responsible, who would take my word over the leader of the coven?

———

"Where in the world have you been?" asked Allie, when I returned to the hotel lobby. "Carey was worried about you."

"Oh, sorry," I said. "I went to Angie's shop to wait for her ghost to show up. Instead, Mina Devlin came in, claiming the shop belongs to the coven now, and booted me out."

"You're lucky that's all she did," she said. "What was she doing there?"

"She wouldn't say," I replied. "I'm also sure whatever hypothetical coven membership I might have had has been extinguished by now, too."

She straightened her hat. "If it makes you feel better, I don't think you're missing out on much."

"I figured, but it's not making this investigation any easier." I released a sigh. "I really thought I'd beat her to finding Angie's ghost. Maybe she'll show up by morning, but now Mina knows…"

"You don't think she's likely to send Angie's ghost away?" she said. "She might be vindictive, but she wants to protect her fellow witches."

"She's also an obstructionist who doesn't want me investigating her coven," I added. "And who breaks into the homes of her fellow coven members after their deaths. She wouldn't tell me why she was there."

Her mouth pressed together. "Be careful, Maura."

All I knew was that I wasn't giving up. I wasn't a quitter by nature, and the detective's belief in me made me reluctant to quit. Unfortunately, I had a grand total of one person left to ask about our vanishing ghost… the Reaper. And given how my usual luck was going, I'd rather not tick him off again. I'd alienated quite enough people this week already.

At least the ghost's room was promisingly silent when I returned to my room and cast a warmth spell to banish the chill from my limbs before putting the bottles I'd swiped from the apothecary on the bedside table.

Mart drifted into the room as I flopped onto the bed. "Who are you? I remember my sister once staying in this room… I remember she promised to let me marathon all the Star Wars movies with her, too."

I lifted my head. "I know I haven't been around much…"

"Because you've been smooching the detective."

"There was no smooching," I said. "A little breaking and entering, though."

"You didn't invite me?" He gave a mock gasp. "I thought we were partners."

I slumped back against my pillows. "Please, lay off the guilt tripping. I've been hiding in the back room of Angie's shop waiting for her ghost to show up for the last hour."

"And did she?"

"What do you think?" I raised my head. "No, instead the very much alive coven leader ambushed me in there and kicked me out. If she *was* the person who banished Harriet's ghost, she's probably already got rid of Angie by now. So at this rate, I'll have to wait until the next victim comes along."

Mart whistled. "So I take it you won't be joining the coven?"

"Definitely not," I said. "Pretty sure I'm blacklisted anyway. Never mind that Mina was breaking and entering, too, and I doubt she had altruistic motives."

"But on the plus side, you don't have to sit through boring council meetings," he said. "Okay, you already dropped that from your life when you picked Reaping over witching anyway. Reapers are much better than witches."

"I'd have had to go to council meetings if I'd become an official Reaper," I reminded him. "You would, too. Just with Reapers and not with witches."

He scoffed. "My choices went up in smoke a long time ago, in case you've forgotten."

"I haven't forgotten." I drummed my fingers on the bed. "I gave up my own choice at the same time, too."

When I'd tied my fate to his, I'd got myself kicked out of my Reaper's apprenticeship and shunned by my former coven at the same time. My brother and I had almost been in a similar position, but I was the one who'd survived. He was stuck as an eighteen-year-old who few people could see, and while we'd both grown used to his predicament, it didn't make him forget it entirely.

"Never mind," he said, in falsely bright tones. "I'll get over it. Or not, as the case may be."

I never quite knew what to say to him in these situations. He knew my regrets and I wouldn't do either of us any favours if I made this about me, so I said, "I could ask Mina to let you join the coven, but I doubt that will go over well. Unless you really want to learn all about boots and broomstick regulations."

"Over my dead body." He laughed at his own joke, which was my plan, and with that, he was past his funk as soon as it had begun.

"I'm kinda worried it might be over mine," I admitted. "How do you think it would go if I publicly accused the coven leader of committing a crime?"

He floated around in a circle, a pensive look on his face. "Depends on the crime."

"She claimed that the healer's shop was the coven's property and she had every right to be in there," I said, "but I still think it's suspicious that she was sneaking around there at night with no explanation."

"Maybe she wanted a boil-cure potion."

I snorted. "She can't see ghosts, but I bet she can banish them. Luckily, I suspected something like that might happen, so I took care to remove certain items."

He floated up to me. "You didn't... did you?"

"I did." I pushed off the bed and indicated the pilfered bottles on the table. "I might have delayed her a bit, but there's more than one source of banishing spells in town."

"You stole from the coven." He shook his head. "And there I thought you were on your best behaviour to impress Mr Detective."

"I'll put them back when Her Highness stops nosing around the place." I sat back down again. "I didn't expect her to come barging in there at night. On top of that, the ghost in the room next door is probably another one of the coven's victims, but if I mention her name to Mina, she'll probably put *me* on their hit list next."

"Wait, what?" he said. "Our unwanted neighbour is a coven member? Since when?"

"I thought you knew," I said. "She used to be a coven member when she was alive, anyway. Drew and I were going to ask Mina about the circumstances of her death, but then we found the healer's body, and now I've ensured she thinks I'm out to start a war with the coven, I'm not sure I *want* to ask her."

"Then I'll find out," he said. "I'm sure one of the other ghosts will know how she died."

I lifted my head. "You'd do that?"

"Why not?" he said. "If it means I don't have to stick around here to listen to her wailing next door, I'd be more than happy to. *If* you keep up your end of the bargain, anyway."

"I appreciate it," I told him. "Really."

If we found out the ghost's identity and the circumstances of her death, we'd be one step closer to the truth—without inadvertently starting a war with Mina Devlin.

If it wasn't already too late for that.

Mart and I stayed up late holding our promised movie marathon, after which he went to ask the other local ghosts about our new neighbour. He wasn't back by morning, so I met Drew and we headed to the hospital to speak to Cathy again.

The new coven healer wouldn't be thrilled to see us, but that was too bad. Maybe I could get some more clues from her about Harriet's death, as well as Angie's, but I had to be careful who I told, given what'd happened to the former healer. And especially after Mina's mysterious appearance in Angie's shop. I decided not to mention that to Drew, given that I'd been the person who'd had the least right to be there out of the pair of us and it wouldn't exactly endear me to the rest of the local police force if I mentioned I'd skirted on the wrong side of the law.

Didn't mean I thought Mina Devlin was the slightest bit innocent, but I'd just have to be sneakier next time.

The detective and I entered the hospital to find Cathy

in the same room as before, where she reacted to our appearance with a sigh and an eye-roll.

"You again?" she said, stirring one of the ever-bubbling cauldrons around her. "Might have escaped your attention, but our last healer died this week, and now the entire coven is mobbing me asking for advice. This is the first free minute I've had in two days."

"I'm aware she's dead," I said. "That's what we came to ask you about."

She groaned. "You think I killed her. As if my week wasn't bad enough already. Sometimes I think I'd rather go to jail than deal with another coven member who's incapable of picking out their own herbal recipes."

"As her successor, you should have been aware you'd be a potential suspect," said Drew, not unkindly. "That doesn't mean I think you did it, but I'm going to have to ask a few questions."

She swore under her breath. "Fine, but please don't take too long."

"When was the last time you saw Angie?" I asked.

"The day I got the position," she said promptly. "She came here to congratulate me. I've been run off my feet ever since."

"Who told you Angie died?" the detective asked.

"Mina did," she responded. "The coven leader would have been the first to know."

"Because we called her," I said. "We went to visit Angie early that morning, and we found her body. Did she not mention that?"

"No, but I didn't ask." Her brows rose. "You're the one who found her? Really?"

"We both did," said Drew. "I called Mina over to her

shop right away, and we've already talked to all the witches who've had contact with her. Except for you."

"Fair enough," she said. "Look, I haven't even seen my own house much this week, and I can't even wrap my head around the fact that she's dead."

"Who, Angie?" I said.

Cathy rubbed her eyes. "I'm too tired to even think, but there's no time for me to stop."

"You shouldn't have to work yourself to death," I said. "Why would the coven members come to you instead of going to the apothecary themselves?"

"Not everyone is a healing expert," she said. "It's not a common gift at all, and with two of the other gifted healers in the coven dead within a week, people think I'm the only option."

That sounded plausible enough. Most witches had one dominant gift and healing wasn't the most common. I was the only witch I knew who didn't have one, but the universe presumably thought my Reaper powers were more than enough to make up for it.

"Doesn't mean they can't do anything for themselves," said Drew.

"Maybe not, but not everyone was thrilled that I got the position," she said. "It wouldn't be a great start to my new job if I spent the week turning people away who need my help. I volunteered for this, but I didn't expect the only other expert healers around to die right after I got the job."

"There are really so few of you," I said. "Like Harriet. I guess her death didn't help matters, either?"

"No, it didn't," she said. "Any progress with your investigation into her death?"

"We confirmed her ghost didn't visit Lisa," I added. "She only came to you. Are you sure it was all about the healing position?"

And not, for instance, because she'd killed her?

"Sounded like it," she replied. "I don't know what she was thinking, but her mind was fixed on the job she lost. I think it was on her mind when she died, and that's why she came here."

"What was her general mood?" I asked. "Was she angry about her death?"

"She was angrier about losing the position of healer, I'd say," she said. "She kept ranting about it. Going on about how Mina was biased against her, that sort of thing."

"She mentioned the coven leader?" I said casually.

"Well, yes," said Cathy. "Mina is the one who chose me, after all. I ended up putting on an earplug charm until she left."

"Did you know she spent a lot of time with Angie?" I asked. "Studying for the test?"

"Yes, I did," said Cathy, in sour tones. "Mostly because she kept switching out her shifts and leaving the rest of us to pick up the slack. That's one reason I was already taking on a ridiculous workload before she died and made it even worse."

Hmm. That might be a motive for murder... or not. Cathy wouldn't have voted to make her own life more difficult, surely.

"What was she like at work, then?" asked the detective. "Before her death?"

She shrugged. "Distracted. Studying all the time and

barely paying any attention except in life or death scenarios."

"Was she really not bothered about Maxwell's cheating?" I asked. "I mean, they were living together."

"You're not going to let this drop?" She looked between us, her lips pursed. "Look, I didn't know her personally. We weren't friends. But I did overhear her talking on the phone when she left her shift, and sometimes... I got the impression she was talking to a guy, and not Maxwell."

"Come again?" I said.

She drew in a breath. "Maxwell wasn't the only one who was seeing someone on the side during the last weeks of their relationship together. Harriet said so when I saw her ghost. She kept saying she had to apologise to him. But I guess she didn't end up doing that."

"Harriet was cheating, too?" That changed things—or not. It certainly added another dimension to the puzzle that was Harriet's life, though. "For how long?"

"No idea," she said. "I think Maxwell suspected, but he's not bright, and he was too fixated on his own affair. I reckon that's why it took so long for both of them to do anything about it."

"Makes sense." But there were still a fair few gaps in the story. Like what exactly had led to the couple finally deciding to split up. "Who was she cheating on him with, do you know?"

"Archie."

"Who's that?"

"A wizard," said Drew. "He was one of the wizards who was at the inn, in fact."

I turned to him. "Not the ones who found her body?"

"The very same."

"Whoa," I said. "He didn't admit it when we questioned him, did he?"

"Perhaps he didn't want to taint her memory," said Cathy.

Or perhaps he had something else to hide.

Drew caught my eye, clearly picking up on my thoughts, and nodded. "I'll certainly be speaking to him again."

"Might he have feared retaliation from the coven?" I asked. "Some of the wizards seem scared of Mina."

"Can you blame them?" said Cathy. "She pretty much threw them out of her office when they asked to set up their own coven."

"Why?" I asked. "What's her issue, anyway? It's not like they would have had any effect on her position as coven leader."

Having one single coven wasn't unusual for a small community, but it still struck me as a bit of an over the top reaction on her behalf. It wasn't like Archie and the other wizards were doing any harm, and it sounded like Mina had a screw loose. Not that I hadn't already suspected that was the case, based on what I'd seen of her.

"That's exactly what she thinks," she said. "You're either in the coven or out, and she's not keen on any rivals getting in the way."

"And how do you feel about that?" asked Drew.

She shrugged. "I'm a healer. This is what I do. I don't get involved in any other drama. If the wizards want to set up their own coven, they're welcome to, but Archie is a few twigs short of a broomstick anyway."

I stifled a laugh. I appreciated her honesty, yet I still hadn't entirely bought her alibi.

"I have one last question," I said. "Do you know why Harriet might have visited Angie's shop the night she died? If not to talk about the position of coven healer?"

"To borrow some herbs?" she said. "I don't know. Maybe she knew everyone kept bothering me and decide to take matters into her own hands. I don't ask her business."

That was probably the closest to an answer I'd get without admitting I suspected the coven leader of being up to no good. It seemed Cathy was keeping secrets from her anyway, but I hadn't entirely removed her from the suspect pool, either.

"Thanks for your time," said Drew.

We left Cathy to her potions and walked out of the hospital into the street, where a few raindrops were beginning to fall from the overcast sky.

"Interesting," I said. "So they were both cheating at once, were they? I guess that explains why she and Maxwell happily drifted apart."

I'd pretty much struck him and Lisa off the suspect list, but as for the wizards at the inn? What had possessed Archie to pretend he hadn't known Harriet at all? That seemed suspect, to say the least. I had to admit I'd never considered any of them might have had a hand in her death, but that didn't make them innocent. Had Harriet been on her way to meet him when she'd died? Why had he lied?

Drew pulled out his phone. "It's almost lunchtime. Archie and the others will probably be at the inn, and we can question them again, if you like."

"You read my mind."

We turned the corner of the street and made our way towards the bridge.

"I think we should ask the wizards if they knew Angie," I said to him. "And find out if they have an alibi for her death. I still reckon the same person who killed Harriet killed Angie, too."

His brow wrinkled. "I can't see why one of them would murder the former healer. They had almost no contact with her, as far as I'm aware."

"Unless they were covering their tracks," I said. "Harriet and the healer spent a lot of time together, especially in the last week or so. Maybe Angie figured out who killed her, and they bumped her off before she could reveal the information publicly."

"Did any of those wizards look capable of brewing up a complicated poison?" he queried.

I considered this. "I guess not. Unless she already brewed it and left it lying around, but one of them might have ended up poisoning himself."

Archie had been among the wizards who'd found Harriet's body, though. I couldn't ignore that connection, nor his inexplicable lapse in mentioning his affair with her. Those things put together painted a picture that didn't look good for the wizards, to say the least.

All the same, the image of Mina Devlin's face kept coming to mind, and a not-insignificant part of me wanted to confront as well. She must know everything that went on within her coven, yet she seemed to be doing absolutely nothing to solve the murder of the former healer. She'd even refused to cooperate with the police.

And I thought I was inept at dealing with people.

We entered the restaurant, where the lunchtime crowd was on their way in. Within ten minutes, a familiar group of wizards arrived, talking raucously amongst themselves.

"Which one is Archie?" I asked.

Drew made a beeline for a wizard who wore a long grey cloak and matching hat and looked altogether more alert than he had the night he and the others had levitated Harriet's body out of the river.

"Excuse me." Drew stepped out in front of him. "You're Archie, right?"

The wizard looked startled. "Something wrong, detective?"

"New information has come to light concerning Harriet's death," he said. "I need to ask you some questions. We won't keep you for long."

His face fell. "Seriously?"

"Like I said, it won't take long."

His friends watched and muttered among themselves as Archie sloped after us into the inn's lobby. Not the most private place for a chat, but the rain had started in earnest and the wizards would only be here for their lunch break. That meant we needed to be quick. At least the only people around were the resident ghosts, who departed when I gave them a warning look.

"What is it?" asked Archie.

"We found out that you and Harriet were involved in a relationship prior to her death," I said. "You didn't mention that when we last spoke to you."

His shoulders slumped. "I… I didn't know how to bring it up. It felt disrespectful to her memory."

"It's still evidence, though," added the detective. "I'm

sure you understand why I have to ask you a few more questions."

He gave a frantic nod. "All right. Um, the truth is, it was a fling. It didn't really mean anything. I think she knew that Maxwell guy was cheating, and she wanted to get back at him, but she was more focused on that coven healer position anyway."

"Was she on her way to meet you the night she died?" I asked.

"If she was, she didn't tell me," he said. "I was on a night out with my mates, that's all. Didn't expect to find her like that. I was here all evening. Ask anyone."

"When was the last time you saw her alive?" queried the detective.

His forehead scrunched up. "Let's think… maybe two days before she died. We usually met at my place, but after her ex moved out, she usually invited me to hers. It was easier that way."

"You never met him?" I asked.

"Not in person, no," he said. "She talked about him, though. Said she planned to break things off, but it was complicated, what with the house and everything."

"So that's why he stayed," said Drew.

He shrugged. "I guess. We didn't know one another, so I can only go by what she told me."

"Did she mention he was cheating, too?" I asked.

"Oh, she knew," he said. "You don't think *he* killed her? Because I doubt he did. He already had what he wanted. Lisa did, too."

"Was Harriet acting oddly before her death?" I asked. "The last time you saw her?"

"Odder than usual?" he said. "I mean, she'd been buried

in books for weeks, trying to prove herself to the coven leader and get the position of healer. She was obsessed, you know what I mean?"

"I think I do," said the detective. "What about Angie? The former healer?"

"Her?" he said. "Oh. She died, right? This week. I heard."

"Murdered," I said, and watched the last of the colour drain from his face.

"Oh." He sagged on his feet like a balloon deflating. "You think I did that? I don't even know how she died."

"Poison," I said. "Have you been living under a rock for the last week? She was poisoned with herbs from her own shop."

"Oh." His expression cleared. "If it was poison, then I couldn't have done it."

"How so?" said Drew.

"I don't know one herb from the other. Only way I might have poisoned someone is by accident with my cooking." He gave a nervous laugh which rapidly petered out.

"Have you spoke to the coven leader this week?" I said. "I know some of you want to start your own coven…"

"That's more Bernard's idea," he said. "What does that have to do with anything?"

Nothing. Except for Mina Devlin's apparent stranglehold over the witches and wizards in town. "I just think it odd that there's only one coven and one healer to go with it. Cathy seems snowed under with work. Have you seen her?"

"Cathy?" he said. "Oh, the new healer. Nope. I didn't

know her, though Harriet talked about her a fair bit. We never crossed paths."

"What did Harriet say about her?" I asked. "She talked about her a lot?"

"Sure," he said. "She said that Cathy was less talented as a healer, but she expected her to get chosen because Mina always picks someone she personally likes."

"I wasn't under the impression she liked anyone," I commented.

He grimaced. "The whole coven is scared of crossing her. Everyone is. But she didn't like Harriet, so she never had a shot at being picked. That's what she told me."

"Then why try?" I felt the detective's eyes on me, and I knew I'd gone off script, but I still wanted to hear what he had to say. "Why did she try for the position, then?"

"I dunno, it was an obsession, like I said." He shrugged. "Maybe she thought if she studied hard enough, she'd be in with a chance of proving Mina wrong. Do you really think Harriet was murdered?"

"I didn't at first," I admitted, "but then someone killed Angie the night after we visited and questioned her about the last time she saw Harriet alive. That suggests they had a reason to want to quieten her."

His eyes widened. "Why?"

Why indeed.

"Would your friends have anything to add to your story?" asked the detective.

"Maybe. I dunno." He frowned. "I'm not a suspect in Angie's death, am I?"

"Depends if you have an alibi for late Tuesday night," I said. "Do you?"

His expression cleared. "Oh, I was here at the inn.

Then I went home, and I could barely walk in a straight line. Bernard can back me up. So can my other friends."

"I'll have to check with him," said Drew.

"Sure." He nodded, edging towards the glass doors to the restaurant. "But none of us did it. We liked the old healer and we didn't have any reason to pick a fight with the coven."

I was inclined to believe him, but I went with Drew into the restaurant and found Archie's friends at the bar. There, Drew launched into questioning each of them to confirm the wizard's presence here at the inn at the estimated time of Angie's death. Not that we knew for certain, since my Reaper senses had chosen to stay quiet for reasons I had yet to figure out.

Bernard, the wizard who'd pulled Harriet's body out of the river, looked especially uncomfortable. He fidgeted more and more the longer the questioning went on. Finally, he said, "Did Mina send you?"

"No, of course not," I said. "Why?"

He shrugged. "I dunno, I'd just rather go to jail than deal with her wrath, so if you're going to arrest me, get it over with."

"Nobody is getting arrested," said Drew. "Unless, that is, you have something to hide, concerning Harriet or Angie's deaths."

Bernard was quiet for a moment. "Not exactly, but... I never told you that I saw weird markings on Harriet's body when we pulled her out of the river. And I don't think the police noticed, or anyone else, either."

"Like what?" I said. "What kind of markings do you mean?"

"I don't know," he said. "They were like... symbols,

written on her hands. I wasn't paying too much attention. I was in shock, to be honest. I didn't think it might be important until later on."

"Did anyone else see?" I looked among the others.

"Um," said Archie. "Yeah, now that you mention it, I did."

I turned to Drew. "Didn't you see?"

"No." His brow furrowed. "Are you implying the marks were magical in nature?"

"Some spells use runes which are only visible to wizards or witches," I said. "Didn't you examine the body?"

"The coven took her body away," said Archie. "I thought they were going to look into it."

"Without telling the police?" I said.

You'd think Mina would want to cooperate with the police if she wanted to find the killer, but if Mina had been the one who'd taken Harriet's body away, perhaps her secrecy had been for a reason.

To be honest, I was starting to run out of excuses to believe she was innocent. But how could I go about accusing her? I needed more proof than I already did, and what I did have was tenuous at best. As for the detective, I wouldn't let him take the risk on my behalf. Especially as we only had the wizards' word to go on about the markings on her body.

Drew finished up the questioning and left the wizards to their lunch break, while I walked with him into the lobby once again.

There, I turned to the detective. "What do you reckon?"

"Nothing ties Archie or his friends to Angie's death,"

he said. "Their alibis are solid. Even with Harriet's death, it seems unlikely he was involved. Unfortunately, the only person likely to know about these marks on her body is the coven's leader. Especially as it was the coven who took over the funeral and buried her."

"Yeah." Unease skittered down my spine. "We need to figure out how to handle it. If we make enemies of the whole coven, it'll be our necks on the line next."

"I won't act without proof," he said. "I intend to check in with my colleagues and see if they can confirm the markings are worth looking into."

"Good thinking," I said. "I wish I could say I knew what it all means, but I don't. I'm in the dark."

"You and me both," he admitted. "I expected this case to be straightforward, but as soon as the coven got involved, and all this extra information came up…"

"I'm wondering why my Reaper senses only reacted to Harriet's death and not Angie's." Was it simply that I'd been close to the scene of Harriet's death, or was it more to do with the manner in which she'd died? It wouldn't usually make a difference, but with my abilities dormant for so long, I couldn't begin to guess at what had caused their resurgence.

Drew took a step closer to me. "I didn't mean to put pressure on you by getting you involved."

"You didn't," I said. "I wanted to get involved. I just wish my Reaper skills were a little more reliable."

Aside from when they sprang up and inconveniently dragged him into the afterworld, that is.

"They alerted you to the first murder, but not the second," he said. "Right?"

"You've got it," I said. "I don't know whether it was

because I was closer to the scene of the first death or if my Reaper skills were already on full alert because I was wandering around a haunted house at the time. Never heard of that happening, but I'm not exactly a typical Reaper."

"Considering the only other Reaper I know is possibly the most antisocial person I've met, I have to agree with you there."

"Hey, I have the antisocial part down," I said. "Look at how I handled the witches."

"You lasted through a whole meeting with them." He smiled. We looked at one another then. I could see something in his eyes, but I wasn't sure if it was my imagination or not.

"Just kiss already!" yelled Mart from behind him, making me jump.

Drew lifted his head. "Was that your brother, by any chance?"

"You've got it," I said. "I think he might have an update on the ghost."

He'd better. Mart grinned and gave me a thumbs-up, while I shot him a scowl.

"I have to report back to the rest of my team," said Drew, with a glance in my brother's direction. "I'll see you tomorrow, Maura."

M art groaned theatrically when the detective left. "He's got to make a move on you first. I'm on tenterhooks here, and I'm *dead*."

"You're also not helping by interrupting our conversations." I rolled my eyes at him. "Go on, give me the update on the ghost."

"Bold of you to assume I have one," he said, "but yes, I have interesting news."

"Like what?"

"I asked the locals about our spirit's death," he said. "Mandy died four years back, and nobody ever came to a definite conclusion about what caused her death. And get this... she was one of the hopefuls for the job of the coven's healer at the time."

My heart skipped a beat. "Really? Did the police have any suspects who they thought might have killed her?"

"No," he said. "The coven leader ruled her death an accident."

"The same leader who still runs the coven now?"

Suspicion trickled through me. This might be the evidence I needed. If I could find a way to bring it to the surface, that is, without getting myself into deeper trouble than I already was. I doubted the witches *or* the police would take my brother's ghost's word as proof.

"Yeah, she's been the leader for years," he said. "Since not long after the floods, I heard."

"The ghosts are being talkative, then?"

"Sometimes," he said. "When I ask the right questions, they don't shut up. It's excruciating. Two of them tried to follow me home."

"Now you know how I feel."

"Oi." He put on a mock-wounded look. "I went out of my way to help you, you know."

"And it's appreciated." It was, too. But I was still as in the dark as ever as to what Mina and the coven's deal was. "Was Angie still the healer back then?"

"She was," he said. "Sounds like she didn't react well to her potential successor dying and decided to put off her retirement for a few more years."

Hmm. Unless the former healer had been murdering her apprentices, which seemed unlikely, she was innocent in this and had likely met her end because she'd made the same connection I had. As for why Mandy couldn't remember her own death? That remained a mystery for now, but the coven was certainly full of people who schemed long and hard to get what they wanted. Including, or especially, their leader.

"Maybe I can convince Mandy to tell me what she recalls of her time in the coven," I said. "If Carey's ghost goggles could actually pick up sounds..."

"That'd work if she could remember her death," he said. "Does she?"

"Nope." Which meant I needed to come up with another strategy in the meantime. If I wasn't out of ideas, that is.

I watched as the wizards traipsed out of the restaurant, muttering among themselves.

"Want me to follow them?" asked Mart. "To make sure they aren't plotting murder?"

"Good thinking," I said. "Be careful, okay?"

He snorted. "Those guys couldn't lay a finger on me even if I was alive."

My brother departed, while I went to get ready for my afternoon shift, thinking hard about how on earth I could possibly go about accusing the coven leader of a crime without ending up in deeper trouble myself. Or putting Drew's life in danger. That, I wouldn't do.

I rubbed my forehead. Complicated. Feelings made life complicated, all right.

———

Carey returned from school midway through my shift and set up her work at the same table as usual. Normally I didn't mind being around her, but my brain was stuck on the dilemma of making a stand against the terrifying leader of the local coven without ending up in a grave of my own. Or turned into a tree. Let's face it, witches could be scarier than Reapers when they wanted to be. More imaginative, certainly. There were only so many things you could do with a scythe.

"How's the investigation going?" she asked. "The detective isn't here?"

"No, he had to go back to the office," I said. "After he talked to the wizards again earlier. The ones who found Harriet's body."

"They're still suspects?"

"One of them had a fling with Harriet before her death." I decided not to bring up the markings allegedly spotted on her body. They were in the realm of rituals and dark magic, especially if the detective hadn't been able to see them. As if the case wasn't confusing enough already.

She looked up at me. "Really? Do you think he killed her?"

"As of right now, no," I said. "He has no motive for murdering Angie, either. Plus he has an alibi. All of them do."

"Weird." Her forehead wrinkled. "Are you going to be working on the case over the weekend, then?"

I didn't want to drag Carey into this, either, but a pang of guilt hit me when I saw the pile of notes on haunted houses on the table next to the laptop I'd loaned her. "Want to go on another visit to old Healey House tomorrow?"

Her expression brightened. "Sure. I'm looking at ways to make ghosts more likely to show up. Maybe we can lure them out."

"I doubt any of the books mention bringing a Reaper along," I commented. "We tend to scare off most spirits."

"I thought the town's ghosts didn't mind you now," she said.

"As long as I don't start waving shadows around," I said. "Other than that, it's hard to summon a specific spirit if it isn't someone you personally know. Or if they didn't die recently."

"Still worth trying," she said. "What's up with you? You seem kinda… mopey."

"Mopey? Me?" I frowned. "I guess I've had a frustrating week."

"Is that ghost still bothering you?"

"What ghost?" asked Hayley, passing by with a tray of drinks.

"My new next-door neighbour." I gave an eye-roll. "As everyone knows, I'm a magnet for unwanted spirits."

"You mean the one that kept screaming?" she said.

"You've got it," I said. "Lucky me. And no, I wasn't thinking about her."

"The detective, then?" put in Carey. "Because it sounds like you've spent a lot of time with him this week."

"No." I absently picked up a glass and started polishing it. "I was thinking about how Mina Devlin keeps getting in my way. Two members of her coven are dead, and you'd think she'd want to help the police, not take the case off their hands and refuse to share anything."

Mart's claim that Mandy's death had been treated in a similar manner set alarm bells ringing in my skull, but how could I make an open accusation against her without proof? The case of Amanda Dawson's death had been closed long ago, if there'd ever been one. I'd need to tell the detective everything that'd since been revealed, but he had enough to handle without me dumping another bombshell on him.

"Not if it threatens the stability of the coven," Hayley said. "That's Mina's priority, above all else. Who's this ghost, anyway?"

"A witch who used to be in the coven," I said, not wanting to drag her into this mess as well. "She tried out for the position of healer a few years ago… which seems to be a great way to end up dead."

"Seriously?" Her eyes rounded. "When?"

"I don't know… maybe four or five years ago, I think," I said. "Sounds like our esteemed coven leader shut down that case, too."

"Sounds like her." Hayley frowned at Carey. "Have you spoken to this ghost?"

"Nope," she said. "I can't hear them. The microphone on my ghost goggles isn't on the right frequency yet."

Yet. Magical technology wasn't my strong point, but it seemed to be Carey's. I was actually pretty impressed at some of the things she'd come up with, including a key that opened any door, and I had no doubt that she'd perfect her ghost-recording gear eventually.

"Well, try not to get into a feud with Mina," Hayley said. "My mum argued with her from her deathbed and I doubt that improved things for anyone."

I could imagine, but Mina was hellbent on getting in our way. She'd even confiscated Harriet's notes which she'd left in Angie's shop, which ought to count as evidence, even if the police hadn't been able to find any clues in them. She'd also taken Harriet's body to the coven without noting the marks on it, which was downright suspicious no matter how I looked at it.

Maybe it was time to take the investigation into my own hands.

———

Once my shift finished, I told Carey I was going to get an early night and left the restaurant. Then, instead of my room, I made for the door leading outside.

Mart appeared behind me and floated into step with me. "Where are you going?"

"To nose around the coven leader's office and steal back the notes she confiscated from the police." I tilted my head at him. "Did you follow those wizards? Learn anything?"

"Nope," he said. "Their conversation is as dull as a wart potion, and if any of them committed murder, I'm a pixie."

"Definitely innocent, then?"

"Regrettably so," he said. "Are you sure you want to antagonise Her Grumpiness? What if it turns out she sleeps in her office?"

"Wouldn't surprise me, but it's worth a look around. Coming?"

"Of course."

I also intended to return the pilfered bottles of ghost-banishing concoction where they belonged, so I'd take a detour to Angie's shop, preferably without the coven's leader interrupting me this time around. Next time, she might not let me off so easily.

Mina already thought I was a troublemaker, but then again, I felt the exact same about her. And she'd thrown up too many red flags for me to ignore them any longer. I just needed to make sure she didn't hurt anyone else while I prepared to take her down.

The two of us crossed the bridge over the river, Mart floating at my side.

"I'm heading to Angie's shop first," I told him. "Might have another look around while I'm at it."

"I've got a better idea," he said. "How about I go and have a snoop around Mina's office to make sure there aren't any traps first? So you don't get yourself into trouble. It's not like she can see me even if she's there."

My mouth parted. "Not a bad idea. She can't see ghosts, but she might have other defences up."

"Relax," said Mart. "She won't know I'm there, Maura. Don't worry."

"If you see the Reaper, get out," I told him.

He snorted. "The Reaper? I doubt he's ever set foot in her office."

He probably wasn't wrong, but the last time we'd split up to investigate separately, he'd wound up locked in the Reaper's house and was lucky not to have ended up banished into the afterlife. Mart was more resilient than most spirits, but whoever was behind the killings had already got rid of one ghost. Maybe two, if Angie had even shown up. We barely knew what we were messing with here.

"All right, but if you see anything dangerous, check in with me," I said.

"Likewise," he said. "You're the one with a pulse, remember?"

Didn't I know it. But Reapers were resilient. We had to be.

I walked out into the dark, crossed over the river, then headed for the witches' area of town. There, Mart and I parted ways outside Angie's shop.

"We'll meet up back at the inn," I said. "Give it half an hour. I won't be long."

"Sure." He waved, then vanished down the road towards the coven's headquarters.

I, meanwhile, turned to the apothecary. It was locked, which I should have expected, and a quick check confirmed the lock spell was more complicated than the usual type. But nothing and nowhere was Reaper-proofed.

Shadows floated from my hands, coalesced in front of the door, and I stepped through them, emerging on the other side as though I'd stepped straight through the wooden surface. The dark shop remained shadowed, but no soul was inside it. Living or dead.

Maybe the shop wasn't where Angie's spirit had appeared after all, but there must be something. I walked into the back room and conjured up a light with my wand before returning the jars I'd borrowed to a dark corner in the back. Then I searched for an object which might have been important to Angie, which I could use in my Reaper tracking to pinpoint her ghost.

If any evidence which led to her killer had been here, though, it'd been removed by now. What had I expected, really? The coven leader had already been in here and taken everything of note. I'd been looking in the wrong place.

Despite myself, I crouched down to search behind the desk. My gaze snagged on a book lying on the floor. A notebook with Angie's handwriting on it, which she'd been writing in when I'd first come here. Impulsively, I grabbed it and put it into my pocket. I didn't particularly want to do my Reaper tracking spell here in the shop in case Mina Devlin interrupted me, so I left the shop the same way I'd come in.

I headed back to the inn, my hands in my pockets and my head in the clouds. What had I really been thinking I'd find, anyway? The evidence would have to be pretty major to implicate the coven leader, and she was too clever to leave anything obvious lying around. I'd have to wait and see what Mart said when he came out of her office. I hoped he'd had better luck than I had.

I was halfway across the bridge when something crashed into me from behind, sending me stumbling over the edge and towards the dark currents of water below.

Shadows spilled out, breaking my fall like a sheet of dark glass. I landed, breathless, suspended in mid-air. My head spun with vertigo. Even for a Reaper, that'd been a close one. I hovered, eyes on the bridge, and spotted a dark figure disappear into the distance. How had my attacker got so close without me spotting them? I'd been lost in thought, and I hadn't been cautious enough at all.

Now I stood suspended in the air, one wrong step from falling to my doom. This was a fine mess I'd wound up in. I shuffled forward, willing the shadows to stay intact until I set foot back on the bridge again. Then I halted, my heart sinking. Someone was walking across the bridge. Someone like… Drew Gardener.

The detective looked down at me. "How in the world did you get down there?"

"Reaper trick," I responded. "Hang on. Just let me walk back to the bridge."

"Let me help you." He reached out a hand, and I closed the short distance between us to grasp his hand and stepped back onto the bridge. The shadows folded back in when I touched down on solid ground.

"Thanks." I released his hand, with more reluctance than I'd have preferred. My heart was still hammering a mile a minute. *Someone tried to kill me.* In the darkness, the only person I could see was the detective. Whoever had knocked me off the bridge had long since disappeared into the surrounding streets.

"What happened?" he asked. "Did you go down to the river looking for clues?"

"Nope," I said. "Someone pushed me in."

His eyes widened. "Who?"

"No idea. They got me from behind. Lucky my Reaper powers kicked in, otherwise I'd be going for an unplanned swim." Shivers ran down my arms. I hadn't been in any danger of drowning, but the person who'd pushed me couldn't have known that. Or hadn't cared.

"What were you doing out here alone anyway?" he asked.

I weighed the odds. "I decided to have another look around Angie's shop. Then I walked back, and someone ambushed me. I didn't see their face. They disappeared before I could get a good look."

His eyebrows rose. "You went back to Angie's shop? Alone?"

"I took Mart with me, but we split up."

That was probably a mistake, too, but Mina was aware of my Reaper abilities and she might have caught me if she was lurking around her office at night. Then I'd have had difficulty defending myself without winding up in deeper trouble.

The detective frowned. "I wish you'd told me you were leaving the inn. It's not safe for you to wander around alone at night."

"I assumed you were back at the office," I said. "Besides, I didn't want you to become a target."

"This is my job," he said. "Investigating Angie's

murder. What were you going to do, then? Summon her ghost in your room?"

I bristled at his tone, which echoed the annoying detective I'd first met rather than the man I'd come to know over the past few weeks. "There's no reason to make fun. I know this isn't my job. As everyone keeps reminding me, I'm not even qualified to join the coven."

"That's not what I—" He broke off. "Look, I wouldn't normally have involved you in the investigation as long as I did, but I assumed you'd tell me everything."

"So I'm being dismissed." My voice came out brittle, my hands shaking from my brush with death. "Look, I'm a Reaper. You needn't fear for my safety. You, however, are human, and two people have died this week already."

"That came out wrong," he said. "Maura, I—"

The sound of drunken singing interrupted us. A group of wizards came out of the inn, pursued by an irritated-looking Hayley, and began weaving their way across the bridge. I really didn't want to go for another swim, so I muttered a goodbye and dodged my way through the crowd.

At the inn, I found Mart hovering in the lobby.

"There you are," said Mart. "Where were you?"

"Drowning in the river," I said. "Thanks for checking up on me."

"Hey, don't look at me," he said. "You told me to meet back here. I didn't know I was supposed to be your body-guard. Who tried to drown you?"

"Sorry," I murmured. "I don't know who it was. I didn't see them up close. I didn't find anything in Angie's shop that would implicate anyone in her death, so I grabbed something of hers and then left."

The near-death experience had rattled me more than I'd expected, and now I felt guilty for snapping at Drew on top of it all. How had I expected him to react to me nearly falling to my death from a bridge?

"Now probably isn't a good time to tell you I couldn't get into Mina's office, is it?" Mart said.

I groaned. "Why not?

"I couldn't get past the door," he responded. "It's ghost-proofed. She put herbs all over the place, I think. No spirit could get in."

"Seriously?" She couldn't possibly have known I was going to send Mart there, right? But maybe she wanted to keep Angie's ghost out… or Harriet's.

Fishy. Definitely fishy.

"Unfortunately," he said. "It's a shame, given the ominous-looking book she left open on the desk."

"A book?" I asked. 'What did it say?"

"No idea," he said. "I couldn't read the title from that far off, but it looked pretty dodgy to me. Weird symbols all over the pages."

Weird symbols. Like the ones on Harriet's body? If I couldn't get my hands on the book, though, there was no proof within reach. "I wish you'd come back the same way as me. Then you might have caught the person who tried to kill me."

"Yes, I would have," he said. "Who'd have tried to do you in?"

"You think I know?" I said. "Good job I got my shadows out in time. It's too cold to swim."

He pulled a face. "Maybe I should have gone alone."

"Don't forget the person doing this is as dangerous to ghosts, too." They'd probably only avoided hurting him because they couldn't see him, but they could see me, and now I'd put a neon target on my head.

"Yes, I know," he said. "You don't need to lecture me, not after you almost got yourself drowned. Didn't the detective come to help you out?"

"He did." I suppressed a sigh. "But I couldn't deal with him being condescending, so I left him. I don't understand why he got me involved to begin with if he was only going to get under my feet."

"Isn't it obvious?" said Mart. "He likes you, and he was looking for excuses to spend time with you."

"Until I wrecked his investigation."

"I wouldn't say you wrecked it. You just destroyed it a little."

"Not helping."

"You also nearly died," he added. "Don't do that."

"I'm more resilient than you know," I said. "I can't actually drown. I just panicked."

"I know you can't drown," he said. "You should have told the detective that."

I groaned. "He'd have still found a way to reprimand me for going off alone. I don't need you getting on my case as well as him."

"You'll see." He floated away through the wall, leaving me alone in the lobby.

Great job there, Maura.

I made for the stairs, debating whether to talk to Mandy again or not. At the rate I was going, I'd scare her off, so I was better off waiting until morning.

I trudged up to the first-floor corridor, where Carey ambushed me on the way to my room, snapping me out of my thoughts.

"Maura," she said. "Come, quickly."

"What is it?"

I hurried after her, down the corridor. The door to my room lay open, as did the neighbouring one. My suitcase lay open, my possessions scattered around the floor. The room next door was in a similar state. As though they knew someone else was in there—

Oh, no.

I took it back. Things most definitely *could* get worse.

The ghost had gone.

13

I sat alone at a table in the restaurant the following morning, nursing a mug of coffee and trying not to feel like the universe was crashing down on my head.

"What's up?" Allie joined me. "I'm sorry about your room."

"That's the least of the problems I've had this week," I said. "Whoever trashed my room also got rid of the ghost, and to be honest, I'm more annoyed about that than the room."

"They got rid of her, but not by banishing her," said Allie. "I looked around the room, and there weren't any herbs in there. Whoever broke into the room only scared her off. She might still be around."

"They might as well have banished her," I said. "I haven't seen her since, and besides, she was already terrified of people. She probably won't be able to speak at all if I ever find her again, much less tell me anything about her death."

"Maybe Drew can help you," she said. "How're things with the detective, anyway?"

I groaned. "I think I insulted him when I didn't let him come with me to nose around Angie's shop yesterday, and then nearly got myself thrown in the river."

Her eyes widened. "Thrown in the river?"

Oops. Why couldn't I seem to stop running my mouth off lately?

"I didn't want to worry you or Carey," I said, "but it was when I was on my way back here. Someone pushed me off the bridge."

Her forehead creased. "Maura, you should have reported it to the police."

Yes. I should have. "I got back here and then everything went to hell again. Besides, it's not like I saw who did it. The detective caught me there and I assume *he* reported it, but I took off before we could get to that point."

"Someone tried to hurt you, Maura," she said reproachfully. "Someone who deserves to be held to account."

"Did anyone from here leave the restaurant around the time it happened?" I asked. "Because they must have been within walking distance."

That, or they'd followed me from Angie's shop. I hadn't been nearly careful enough at watching my back. But if it'd been a witch, they wouldn't have needed to be standing behind me to push me. Given how far off the person had seemed to be, maybe they *had* used magic to do it. Didn't mean I knew who was responsible, though.

"Not that I saw," she said. "I do think you should talk to Drew about this."

"It's fine. I'm a Reaper. Theoretically, I could fall off a building and be fine. Ghosts are more of a danger to me than living people are."

I wasn't exaggerating. The retired Reaper had lost his apprentice in a torrent of ghosts who'd shown up following the flood in town two decades ago, but the rest of us were generally more resilient when it came to attempts on our life from living people. I'd thought the detective knew that, but even knowing the theory didn't make the reality any easier to deal with. I'd have freaked out if I'd seen him dangling above the river with nothing below him but darkness.

"Talk to him." She rose to her feet and walked to the bar. "You'll thank me later."

"I'll talk to him." What I'd say, though, I still didn't know.

Did he really want to date me, or just the person he thought I was? As a human, I was all for it, but as a Reaper, I wasn't sure I could give him what he wanted or needed. The detective struck me as the kind of guy who wanted someone steady, someone who'd stick around. Someone who didn't sneak around in the shadows and derail his murder investigations.

I'd only make things worse if I set the coven leader against the pair of us, but who else was willing to do anything about her? He'd definitely be horrified if I went after her alone, but she'd already covered up at least one death, not to mention removed all the evidence from the crime scene. There was no telling what she might do if things escalated to the point that she felt her coven was threatened.

Hayley walked past the table, startling me out of my reverie. "Hey, Maura."

"Hey." I managed a wan smile.

"I heard what happened," she said. "With the ghost up in your room. Someone banished her?"

"Or chased her off," I said. "Just when I thought I was getting somewhere with her."

"In what way?" she asked. "I never asked—what was her name? The ghost?"

"Amanda Dawson," I said, figuring there was no harm in telling her.

Her expression froze. "Are you sure?"

"Yeah… why?" I rose to my feet, adrenaline spiking. "Wait, you knew her?"

"Not personally, but everyone in the coven at the time heard about her death," she said. "I didn't know it was that recent."

"Do you know why she'd come here, and not wherever she lived?" I asked.

She shook her head. "I didn't know her well, but I do remember Mina shutting down the investigation into her death. Have you asked her about it?"

"No, because Angie died before I had the chance to," I said. "And everyone else on the committee within the coven does what she says, so they're likely to tell tales on me to her if I start probing into a years-old case."

"If it helps, I won't tell tales," she said. "If her ghost remembers how she died, this could change everything?"

"She doesn't," I said. "How did she die?"

"She drowned," she said. "There was a fuss about it at the time because it didn't look like an accident, but Mina managed to shut down the rumours after it became clear nobody was going to be able to find out who did it, and it was only turning the coven members against one another."

"Sounds familiar." Just look at how Mina had reacted to the two recent deaths. How many more scandals had she swept under the carpet?

More to the point... *drowned.* In the river, I was betting. Her death and Harriet's were linked more closely than I ever would have guessed.

"Are you two okay?" Allie walked past again, waving her wand to set the vacated tables on either side of us.

"Yeah, we were just talking about the ghost in my room," I explained. "Turns out Hayley knew her."

"Not well," Hayley said. "I was in the coven at the time, though, and I remember the killer was never caught."

"Mina Devlin shut down the investigation," I told Allie. "Took away her body before anyone could look at it."

"Not quite," said Hayley. "I mean, several people saw her body before the burial. That's what tipped them off that it wasn't an accident. There were these... markings, on her body, they said."

My stomach lurched. "Markings? Like what?"

"I don't know," she said. "Mina shut down the case pretty fast. The same didn't happen with Harriet, did it?"

"The exact same," I said. "Markings and all. Though the only people who saw the marks on her hands were the wizards who pulled her out of the river, and they were all drunk at the time. They didn't think anything of it."

She paled. "Are you sure they were telling the truth?"

"I think they were," I said. "They didn't know what the markings were, but Mina took the body away for a reason."

"Tell the detective," said Allie. "Don't go off alone, Maura. That clear?"

I watched her walk away, my head spinning. The detective. Had he been chief of police back then? No, he hadn't, but the police were bound to have the records of Amanda's death. I ought to have looked into it sooner.

One thing was certain: I needed to find Drew and hope he forgave me. If he had the details of the case, he might also have something that belonged to Mandy when she was alive. If I could get my hands on the right tools, I'd be able to lure her ghost back and find out her side of the story. In detail, this time, regardless of what it meant for Mina and the coven.

"Tell you what," said Hayley. "I'll take over your shift, if you like. Give you the chance to meet Drew and see what you can find out."

"Thanks." I smiled. "I appreciate it."

I fired off a message to the detective. Then I waited.

———

Drew met me in the lobby twenty minutes later. I'd worried something would have come up at work or that he'd taken our minor spat yesterday to heart, but here he was, as though nothing had happened at all.

He walked in through the front door. "How're things?"

"Pretty lousy, actually," I said. "Someone ransacked my room and chased the ghost off."

"When was this?" he asked.

"Right after I got back last night," I said. "And I was already having a crappy day."

"No kidding," he said. "I'm sorry I snapped at you. I

panicked when I saw you fall off the bridge. It slipped my mind that you were more resilient than most people."

"I'm sorry, too," I said. "I should have mentioned I can't actually drown."

"I know you can't, but that doesn't mean it doesn't worry me when you take risks," he said. "This case... it's already led to two ghosts disappearing."

"Or three." I hadn't even thought to look for Angie's ghost yesterday, though I'd initially planned to use the notebook I'd taken from her shop to track her down. I'd been too distracted by Mandy's disappearance and the attempt on my life. I'd need to deal with that, too, once I had a spare moment.

"Was the ghost from the inn banished, then?" he asked.

"Not with magic," I said. "She was chased off. But get this—Hayley remembers Mandy's death, a few years ago. Will the police still have records? Her name was Amanda Dawson."

"Right, you told me," he said. "It slipped my mind."

"Mine, too, but I was just talking to Hayley and it sounds like Amanda died the same way Harriet did," I explained. "Apparent drowning, but marks were found on her body. What're the odds that the same markings were found on Harriet, too? I think you should ask for the records, if the police have them."

"They'll want to know why I'm dragging up an old case, but I'll try," he said.

"Apparently, the coven leader buried the whole thing," I said. "Literally. She didn't want the coven to break apart in arguments. Sound familiar?"

He gave a slow nod. "Yes, but we need to tread carefully. Mina has already been at my office at least once per day since Angie's death, asking for updates."

"Of course she has." Yet another complication I didn't need. If she knew everything the police did, she might well have taken steps to hide any incriminating information already. She'd certainly removed evidence from the scene. And as for the book Mart claimed to have seen in her office last night...

"Also," I added, "if you have records of Mandy's death, would you be able to find something that belonged to her when she was still alive? Because if you can, I'll be able to track her down, wherever she's hiding."

Assuming she hadn't been banished for good, that is. Someone had wanted her out of the way, and the ghost was so easily scared that the person who'd got rid of her hadn't even needed to be able to see her to terrify her into leaving.

Drew and I reached the small red brick building which housed the local police department, and I waited in the reception area while the detective went looking for the files on Amanda Dawson's death. I'd never actually been here before, since he always came to the inn instead. Which was a sign Mart would have pointed out as being so obvious it might as well be wearing Marie's pink hat and singing karaoke.

"Nice place, this," said Mart, as though my thoughts had conjured him up.

"There you are." I kept my voice low in case anyone was listening in. "Did you follow me?"

"Obviously," he said. "I thought you were with the detective, but it looks like he's ditched you instead. Why are you here?"

"To find out the records of our ghost's death," I said. "If they have anything of hers here, so much the better. I need to track her down."

"Why would you want to do that?" He pouted. "I was almost considering coming back to your room now she's no longer around."

"She was killed in the same way Harriet was," I whispered. "There were marks on her body, too. And the case was never closed. If she can reveal who did it…"

"Case closed." He flew around the office, and several papers rustled in the faint breeze stirred up by his presence. "So… do you already have a suspect?"

"Yeah, I do," I murmured. "But it's someone who won't take kindly to an open accusation."

"You think it's the coven leader."

I dipped my head. "Why else would she be hellbent on covering up both deaths at once? No other explanation makes sense. So we need evidence, and we need to figure out how to get the ghost to testify in a manner which removes all doubt."

"Wise idea," he said. "Except nobody aside from you can see or hear her."

"I know." It would have helped if we'd found some kind of evidence in Mina's office, but I'd need to get past her defences in order to drag it out into the open. Even then, it might not be enough to convict the most powerful witch in town.

The sound of a door opening made me turn around. The detective was back. "I have the files."

"And…?"

He drew in a breath. "It's as you said. Amanda Dawson was believed to have drowned, but the facts didn't add up.

Amanda Dawson's family wanted to push for answers, but the leader blocked anyone outside the coven from investigating."

Of course she did. "Did you get any statements from the family, or... or anything to suggest where the markings came from?"

"No," he said. "Her body washed up on the bank of the river. I couldn't find any more details than that. The other officers either weren't around at the time or don't remember much about the case."

"Depends if Mina decides to tell us, then." I wasn't betting on it. "What about something belonging to Mandy?"

"It seems all her possessions ended up with her close family," he said. "I have her sister's address."

"Ah." I grimaced. "I don't want to drag anyone else into this, but I really do need something that belonged to her in order to find her ghost."

"If you explain, I'm sure she'll be willing to help you," said Drew.

"You're overestimating my people skills." But I didn't see another way to find the ghost, short of sending Mart around town to hassle people, and I'd put him in danger enough times already. Once we had Amanda's ghost back within reach, it was only a matter of time before someone tried to banish her again. This time, for good.

I'd get to the truth before then. I was counting on it.

———

Drew and I reached Mandy's sister's house, which stood on a row of terraces near Harriet's old house. We'd debated over how much to tell her, but in the end, the need for justice had won out. I wanted her to know we planned to help her get to the truth about her sister's death by any means possible.

Drew knocked on the door and a young woman with a heart-shaped face and dark curly hair answered.

"Oh—Detective Drew." Puzzlement flickered through her features. "Can I help you?"

"I apologise for disturbing you," he said, "but we have reason to believe that your sister's ghost is present in town."

"She came to me," I added, as the colour drained from her face. "She showed up at the inn where I'm staying, and we think the recent death of a coven member might be connected with your sister's death, too."

"Harriet Langley?" She leaned on the door frame with one hand, visibly shaken. "You know, I wondered, when I heard about her trying out for the position of coven healer... but I didn't believe it. Didn't want to. I mean, it was years ago."

If Hayley had made the connection, then of course Mandy's sister would have suspected, too, if the news of Harriet's death had dredged up painful memories.

"Her ghost doesn't remember all the details," I told her, "but I did speak to her, and it took me a while to get her name. Can you see ghosts?"

"No." She shook her head. "You spoke to her? How? I've never... never heard of her ghost being seen anywhere before."

"I think she's been hiding," I said. "But the recent case must have jogged her memory about her death, and she came to me because I'm working with the police investigation."

That, and I was a Reaper, but I'd rather not get into that part now.

She shook her head. "You won't find anything. I never did, and I used to visit the river every day after they found her body. Can you see her ghost now?"

"That's the bad news," I said. "Someone scared her away from where she was hiding out at the inn. I can track her down, but I'll need to borrow something that belonged to her, if that's okay. Something important to her, if you have anything."

She gave a nod. "Sure."

She disappeared into the house and ran upstairs, while the detective and I waited downstairs. A minute later, she returned, her eyes puffy, and she handed me a pointed hat embroidered with pink flowers. "This is all I could get. I hope it's okay."

"It should be," I said. "If you have anything more to say about her death, you can tell us in confidence and we won't tell a soul."

"I can tell you what I remember," she said. "They wouldn't let me see her until the day after she died."

"Meaning, Mina wouldn't?" I guessed. *That's the connection.* But what did it all mean? "Do you remember anything else? Did you see her body?"

Her shoulders stiffened. "I wasn't supposed to."

"But you did, right?" I kept my tone as gentle as I could muster. "Were there marks of any sort on her body?"

"There were markings on her... markings on her hands... like runes." She shuddered. "I tried to tell the coven there was something odd about them, but they wouldn't listen. I was positive the marks looked like some kind of sacrificial magic, but I was outnumbered. It was my word against the rest of the coven."

"A sacrifice?" I echoed. "For what?"

Her eyes brimmed with tears. "I wish I knew. Then I might have had a chance of getting closure."

"That's our plan." I held up Mandy's hat. "We're looking for the truth about Harriet's death, and I'll do my best to get answers about Mandy's, too. We'll be in touch when we know more."

"Thank you," she whispered.

As the door closed, I held up the pointed hat. The detective eyed the embroidered flowers on the edge. "You can find her using that?"

"If she's still around, I can." I took in a breath. "You don't have to stay with me."

"But I will," he said. "Don't worry, Maura. I'm here."

Warmth bloomed inside my chest, and a new resolve settled on my shoulders. Time to track down the ghost.

14

Shadows spread outward from my feet, and I held up the hat as the darkness folded around me. Drew didn't make a sound, and while he must be at least a little unnerved, he didn't say a word. I did my best to tune out the world around us and concentrated hard on my Reaper senses, urging them to point me in the right direction. Like the point of an arrow, they led me towards the ghost. So she hadn't been banished. She *had* fled. Straight to…

I lowered the hat. "You've got to be kidding me."

"What?" said Drew. "Where is she?"

"Hiding with the Reaper of all people."

"It's a logical choice," he said. "She came to you because you were a Reaper, right? So it makes sense that she'd choose to hide with the other Reaper rather than anyone else."

I twisted my mouth into a grim smile. "I guess she picked me first because I'm the nicer of the two of us."

Which was worrying, if nothing else. Depending on an

antisocial Reaper like me who'd already alienated the entire witch coven didn't strike me as a good move, but I suspected I was the only person who could handle this for that very reason.

After the detective had returned the hat to Mandy's sister, the two of us left for the cemetery and approached the Reaper's house. I knocked, once, and he answered, the transparent form of Amanda Dawson hovering behind him.

"Come to collect your ghost?" he asked.

"Pretty much," I replied. "Mandy... did you see who chased you off?"

She lurked behind him, her head bowed. "I can't come out, Maura."

"You have to," I said softly. "I spoke to your sister—"

Her head shot up and she released a howl, cut off when the Reaper made a threatening movement in her direction.

I glared at him. "I don't think the tough love approach is going to work here."

"Then try another angle," said the Reaper. "She's your responsibility, not mine."

"How long has she been here?" I asked. "At least a day, right? You still let her stay, despite claiming not to care."

"That's because she's not making any sense," he growled. "Seems to think the whole coven is after her."

My heart sank. "Maybe they are."

Or they would be, if the truth came out. *When* the truth came out. No matter how reluctant she might be to talk, I needed to get the answers from her if I was to stand any chance of bringing justice to the victims. Including her.

"Then get her out of here," he said. "I don't want to be involved."

"Because you clearly have so much else going on in your life." I walked past him towards the ghost, ignoring his grumbling.

The Reaper tried to block my path, only to find his way barred by the detective. I gave Drew a grateful nod, and slipped through the nearest door, finding the ghost hiding in the living room. "Hey, I'm not going to hurt you."

She shrank back. "It's not you I'm worried about."

"I'll help you stay safe," I told her. "Your sister would very much like to get justice for your death, and I think I know what happened."

She didn't make a sound.

"You were sacrificed," I said to her. "Weren't you?"

She made a faint whimpering noise, yet she didn't say a word.

"Someone killed you in a ritual, the same way they did to Harriet," I went on. "Why?"

Her voice dropped to a whisper. "To take my magic. Healing magic... it's the rarest kind, especially within our coven."

So it's true. But why would someone use the same method to kill Harriet after such a long time had passed? Cathy had already told me she hadn't been involved, but she must know something more, even if she wasn't the killer herself.

One thing was for certain: I needed to take this straight to the coven leader. At least with Drew by my side, I wouldn't be alone, because this was going to get ugly no matter what.

"Are you absolutely certain you don't remember anything else?" I asked. "Whereabouts did you die, anyway?"

"In that old house, of course," she said. "Near the river."

"You don't mean Healey House?"

Hang on. The increased reports of ghostly activity had only started within the last two weeks, which coincided with when the position of coven healer had opened up. I'd bet that was what had awakened her. No wonder she'd come after me, since I'd been there that night. It seemed Carey and I had found our ghost after all.

"I didn't see the killer," she whispered. "I was walking alone, and I blacked out with no warning. Then I remember floating in the air and seeing my body below me, and there were runes drawn on my hands. I don't remember anything else. All I know is they wanted my magic."

I drew in a breath. "Okay. I know only a few people can see you. Can you name anyone in the coven who can see ghosts and who Mina is likely to believe?"

"No!" She shook her head more violently. "She's dangerous."

I spotted the Reaper watching me and raised my voice a fraction. "So am I."

If she didn't want to leave, I'd have to get the evidence in another way, but at least now I knew where she was hiding out. Even the coven leader would surely hesitate before attacking the Reaper, if just because of the scythe in his hallway and the potential backlash from striking an Angel of Death, even a retired one.

The Reaper scowled at me as I turned in his direction. "You aren't taking her with you?"

"I have a job to do first," I said. "I'll come back."

He huffed. "I'm not dealing with the coven."

"Look, can you just sit tight for a minute?" I nodded to Drew. "I think we should head back to the hospital."

Understanding crossed his expression. "Stay here. We'll come back."

The Reaper's angry mutters pursued us out the door, but he made no move against Mandy's ghost, for a wonder. Maybe he had something resembling a heart after all. That, or he thought it wasn't worth arguing with me on this one. Whatever the case, I wasn't complaining.

As for the killer, though? Cathy stood out as the one unifying factor in both deaths aside from the coven leader, but I couldn't think who else would have something to gain by this. The coven leader surely didn't need any more magic than she already had, right?

Cathy could see ghosts and Mina had chosen her as the coven's healer. That had to mean she was trusted. But if she *was* the killer—if she'd done the sacrifice in order to gain her powers—then I wasn't sure who else I might choose to argue Amanda's case to Mina Devlin and force her to listen. Unless Carey's microphone suddenly gained the ability to record ghosts, I was stuck.

We reached the hospital and found Cathy in her usual place, surrounded by bubbling potions.

Her eye twitched when she saw us. "What is it this time?"

"Amanda Dawson."

Her eyes widened. "Oh."

"Yeah," I said. "Care to explain?"

Her shoulders slumped. "I don't think you're going to believe me, but I didn't kill her."

"So you didn't know someone in the coven has been performing sacrifices?" I said. "Twice, years apart? The same person who then killed your mentor?"

She grimaced. "I didn't want her to die. And I swear I didn't kill anyone."

"You helped the coven leader cover up the murder, though," I guessed. "Right?"

"I had to," she said, in defiant tones. "If everyone in town had found out, there'd have been an uproar. They'd have torn the coven to the ground and removed her from her position. We'd have fallen apart. So I did it for her, and—"

"And she repaid your favour later down the line by giving you the position of healer," I finished.

I doubted Cathy had had the clout to argue with the coven leader, so she'd felt she had no choice in the matter, but she was far from innocent in this.

She dipped her head. "I didn't get my magic by stealing it from someone else. I never took part in any rituals."

"Just a cover-up," said Drew, the hint of a growl to his voice. "So why would someone do the same to Harriet? If they took one witch's power, that ought to have been enough."

"Unless it wasn't," I said. "Or unless someone found out the truth about Amanda's death."

She fidgeted, stirred a potion with one hand. "Got it in one. Harriet was so determined to get the position of healer that she borrowed every book on the subject."

"Including a book with details of magical rituals to transfer magic from one witch to another," I said, recalling Mart's visit to Mina's office. "And she told Angie in the hopes that she'd help her solve the case. Instead, someone killed her and then poisoned Angie to ensure she didn't tell anyone else."

"You suspected," Drew said to Cathy. "You knew, in fact."

"Who was I supposed to tell?" she said. "The police? You must know how deadly that magic is. There's nothing anyone could have done to stop it."

"I beg to differ," Drew said. "Whereabouts is this book now?"

She hesitated. "I don't have it."

The coven leader does.

She might not be the killer, but she'd helped them cover up by removing the evidence, ensuring that the coven would never be implicated in the dark magic it had unearthed.

But that still left open the question of the killer's identity. Someone in the coven, evidently, given Mina's attempts to cover it up... twice.

"Don't leave," warned Drew. "I'll be back for you later."

As we walked out, he sent a message on his phone.

"Calling backup?" I guessed.

"We might need it." He led the way out of the hospital. "I suppose you know where the book is?"

"I should go to Mina's office alone," I said. "I know what you're going to say, Drew, but she's dangerous and I can only guess what else she might be hiding in there. Besides, I have a few skills up my sleeve. She won't see me."

"If I hadn't seen what you did on the bridge, I might have doubts," he remarked. "But I can't let you do this alone."

"Wait here for backup to arrive," I said. "Don't let

Cathy slip away while my back's turned. I'll be back in half an hour."

He shook his head. "I shouldn't."

"But you will."

Instead of replying, he briefly embraced me. My heart gave an uneven jolt, and I searched his gaze and found nothing there but trust and the knowledge that he believed I could do this.

It was time to find out what the coven leader was really hiding.

———

Alone, I approached Mina Devlin's office. Then I used my Reaper abilities and stepped through the shadows, emerging on the other side of the door. I expected to find the book open on the desk, its owner glaring at me and ready to kill.

Instead, the ghost of Angie the healer looked at me from the other side of the coven leader's desk.

"You," I said. "What—?"

"Why did you come here?" she said. "Fool."

"For the book, what else?" I said. "Mina trapped you in here, didn't she?"

"She had to," she said. "To stop me from stirring up trouble."

"Looks like she's looking for trouble herself," I said. "Considering she left you here unattended. Where is she?"

"How should I know?" she grumbled. "She left me at least an hour ago."

"She thought you'd come straight to me," I surmised. "And then I'd tell the police the truth. Where is the book?"

"Already gone," she said. "Before she trapped me in here."

"Then who has it?"

That was the question, wasn't it? Whoever it was, they'd already chased off Mandy's ghost once before.

"You're a Reaper," she said.

"Half Reaper," I said. "If I get you out of here, can you tell me everything you know?"

She eyed me. "Very well. Harriet was set on becoming coven healer. She borrowed a large number of books from me to study."

"The book of rituals?"

"No," she said. "She got that one from the bookshop."

"The one where her ex worked." There was the other connection. "She must have seen Mandy's body back when she died, or otherwise guessed something was fishy about her death. So she went to you, right?"

"Not at first, but she brought the book to me to ask a few questions," she said. "The ritual is designed for a witch or wizard to take someone else's magic. I don't remember her knowing Mandy particularly well when she was part of the coven, but there were a few rumours at the time, since she'd been the favourite to become coven healer before she died."

That didn't explain who'd killed her or why, but I was almost there. I knew it.

A rapping on the door made me jump and spin around.

"It's me," Drew said from the other side of the door. "Mina's on her way back."

I stepped through the shadows out of the office and

emerged at his side. "Angie's ghost is in there, but not the book of rituals. Someone already removed it."

The detective released a breath. "Maura, I'm going to gather a team and find a way to handle this which doesn't involve us going to war with an entire coven. Word seems to have spread fast. Did you tell anyone at the inn about the case?"

"Except for Allie and Carey?" Wait, I'd also told Hayley.

Hayley, who'd known more about the circumstances of Mandy's death than I'd expected. Who'd left the coven herself.

And who I'd also told about the identity of the ghost next door to my room.

I had to get back to the inn. If I wasn't already too late, that is.

15

I ran back to the hotel, my feet hardly touching the ground. My Reaper speed kicked into gear, and I didn't stop until I skidded to a halt at the front door. The lobby was deserted. That wasn't a good sign. I pushed the door open and entered the restaurant. Equally empty. Even Allie had disappeared.

"Where is everyone?" I remarked aloud. "Carey? Allie?"

A meow sounded, and Casper stuck his head out from under the table.

"Where is she?"

He gave another pitiful meow. I looked around for any signs of life—or ghosts—and spotted one of the regular spirits hovering in the lobby, a teenage boy who usually haunted the restaurant.

"Whereabouts did everyone go?" I asked the ghost.

"They left," he said in a mournful voice. "Allie closed up the place."

"What?" I rotated on my heel, scanning the restaurant.

"Carey wouldn't leave her familiar behind. And Allie wouldn't abandon the restaurant."

"Allie told them to leave," said the ghost of a teenage girl, floating up to join him. "She went to find her daughter. Carey left earlier, with—"

"Hayley."

My heart lurched. Where had they gone? Nobody was in the lobby, not in the games room or the restaurant. I ran for the stairs and pelted up to the first floor, but the door to Mandy's room stood ajar. The ghost was nowhere to be seen, of course.

My own room was equally empty. I turned everything over in search of clues and found the notebook I'd taken from Angie's shop lying on the bedside table. Other than that, nothing remained. Where had Hayley taken Carey— and why? To lure me after her, maybe. Or because she'd come to the same conclusion I had. Her mother probably had, too. So where…?

"Healey House." I swore. "I was supposed to be going there with Carey tonight anyway."

Casper meowed plaintively from beside my ankle. I leaned down to give him a stroke behind the ears. "Will you be okay staying here?"

He shook his head, his whiskers twitching, and trailed after me downstairs and into the lobby. I stepped out of doors and headed towards the bridge over the river, Carey's familiar glued to my side. My heartbeat quickened at the sight of the water surging below, a reminder of my last brush with death. Casper padded alongside me across the bridge, his fur standing on end.

"Don't worry," I murmured to him. "I'll keep you safe."

I hope. Mart was nowhere to be seen either, but there

wasn't much he could have done to help me in this scenario. It wasn't a ghost we faced, not this time.

I descended the slope to Healey House, where Hayley paced in front of the door, her wand in her hand.

"Took you long enough," she said. "Now, are you going to get rid of that ghost or not?"

I stiffened. "What did you do to Carey?"

"She's fine for now," she said. "I only brought her here to make sure you do as I ask."

"That's not going to work," I said. "Mandy's ghost isn't even here. You know she isn't."

"You're a Reaper," she said. "I'm sure you can change that."

I shook my head. "That's not all you want from me. You wouldn't have gone to the trouble of covering your tracks twice in a row if you didn't care whether or not I told anyone you killed her."

"You won't tell anyone." She jerked her head towards the house. "Come in. Carey's waiting for you."

"What is the matter with you?" I hissed at her. "She's a kid. You worked with her for years."

Her mouth twisted. "I had no choice. My mother's death left me with nothing, and the coven didn't want me around. Look, just come in here and I won't have to hurt anyone."

Except for me, I'd wager. I glanced to the side, but Casper was nowhere to be seen. I didn't blame him a bit, but I was fresh out of allies and I didn't dare risk Carey's safety now Hayley had come utterly unhinged.

I followed Hayley into the house, which was as quiet and damp as ever.

"Why'd you sacrifice Harriet?" I asked her. "Why'd you

kill her in the exact same way as you did to Mandy? Were you that certain Mina would cover up for you a second time?"

She didn't meet my eyes. "She doesn't care about anything but the coven's reputation, and she won't have word spreading that anyone inside the coven is practising illegal sacrifices. Besides, I knew nobody else would recognise the markings."

Except for Harriet. She put two and two together and paid the price with her life. "What did you need Mandy's magic for in the first place?"

"To save my mother's life," she said. "I needed the position of coven healer if we were to gain any chance of stopping the cancer from killing her, but by the time I figured out how to get her magic, it was too late."

"You didn't get Mandy's healing magic," I said, the truth dawning on me. "The ritual didn't work, did it? That's why you left the coven and blamed Mina and the others for your own failures."

"The coven did nothing for me." Tears glittered in her eyes, but her jaw was set in defiance. "I tried to go on and put the past behind me, but Harriet insisted on dragging up the case again. When she realised she was sitting on evidence of an unsolved murder, she refused to let it go. It's lucky she only told one person about her discoveries."

"Angie," I finished. "So you decided to poison her when you figured that she'd put two and two together. I guess you pushed me into the river for the same reason."

"I should have guessed a Reaper would be hard to get rid of."

"So you decided to help me instead," I said. "So I wouldn't suspect."

Not until it was too late, anyway. Worse, I couldn't hear a word from behind any of the doors in the house. What had she done to Allie and Carey?

"Like I said, I don't want to hurt Carey or her mother," she said. "I have a spell prepared. A memory charm which will make them forget any of this happened. But before I let them go, I'm going to need you to get rid of the ghost of Amanda Dawson."

"Not the ghost of Angie, too?" I said. "I guess the coven leader already has that in hand. Is she really so scared of letting the police in on coven business?"

"She's scared of being kicked out of the coven leadership," she said. "She worried that the murders would prompt the coven to come under investigation and expose all the crimes she's committed in order to keep her position."

"She won't have it for much longer, one way or another," I said. "Where is she?"

"Does it matter?" She raised her wand. "Go on. Call back Mandy's ghost, and I won't have to hurt anyone. Use your Reaper skills. I know you can."

I shook my head. "I won't."

Her wand waved, and the door flew open behind her. Carey and Allie sat back to back on the living room floor, their hands and feet bound with ropes. Anger spiked within me, and shadows darkened my palms.

"Go on." Her wand flicked, and Carey moaned. "I won't ask you again."

"Damn you." *Think, Maura.* Drew didn't know I was here. He was with the police, preparing to find the coven leader, wherever she was hiding. Mart wasn't around, either. I had one backup plan at my disposal.

I held up my hands, letting shadows fold across the floor until the darkened form of the afterlife filled the area in front of the door. Hayley's eyes widened. "What are you doing?"

"Finding the ghost."

And giving you a good scare, too. I was normally careful to hide this side of my powers, but Carey had seen it before and she trusted me. Hayley, though, paled, and her wand trembled in her hand. "If I find out you're deceiving me—"

A loud meow sounded, and Casper leapt out of the gloom, hissing and spitting. Hayley yelped and dropped her wand on the floor as the yowling familiar crashed onto her head. I seized my chance and snatched up her wand, kicking the door open. Then I ran to Carey's side and crouched down. Her ghost goggles sat at an odd angle on her head, her expression befuddled, but she stirred when I leaned closer. "Maura?"

A blast of air rattled through the room.

"Don't move!" Hayley shouted. Her face was bleeding where Casper had scratched her, but the little cat cowered away from her trembling hand. "I don't need a wand to use magic."

Crap. She must have more skill than I'd thought. If we started a magical duel here, Carey and her mother might get caught in the backlash. Hayley was prepared to kill to get what she wanted, but if I finished her off, the truth might never get out, and the victims would never get closure.

I crouched beside Carey and whispered in her ear. Then I rose to my feet. My hand slid into my pocket, finding Angie's notebook.

"I'll find the ghost," I told Hayley. "But I need you to promise not to move an inch."

Shadows swirled around my feet and spread through the room, revealing a door etched against a blank backdrop. The door to the afterlife. As Hayley stared in mute horror, I used my Reaper senses and stepped through the shadows, emerging in the coven leader's office. At once, I found myself face to face with Angie's ghost.

"Back again?" she said. "Don't you have somewhere more important to be?"

"I'm a Reaper," I told her. "I can be in several places at once, technically speaking. Your murderer is currently threatening me. Care to give me a hand?"

She frowned. "You can't get me out of this office... can you?"

"I can." I stood back, and the shadows folded in around her. "Reaper skills can't be held back by a simple barrier spell. Come with me."

She floated after me into the shadows, and we both emerged in the living room of Healey House. Behind me, Carey whispered to her mother, Casper curled up protectively at her side.

Across the room, Hayley hadn't moved an inch, though she was still bleeding where the cat had scratched her. Her eyes widened at the sight of the healer's ghost. In the afterlife, anyone could see the dead. The chill in my hands warned me that I'd overstretched my powers, but as long as I held up, everyone would stay alive.

"You said you'd find Mandy's ghost," Hayley said. "You lied. That isn't her."

"You poisoned me," said Angie, accusingly. "You did as much wrong to me as you did to the girl."

"You were poking your nose into the wrong business." Her face flushed, her mouth pinching. "If you'd just left it alone—"

"You murdered Angie," I said to Hayley. "The same way you killed Mandy and Harriet. Do you deny it?"

"No, but—who cares, anyway?" she burst out. "Mina Devlin did worse. She only cares about the coven, and I bet I'm not the only person she's covered for."

That was all the proof I needed. I gave a faint nod, and Allie rose to her feet, her wand in her hand. Carey did likewise, her familiar at her side.

"How—" Hayley's eyes widened as she flew backwards into the wall. Recovering, she lunged at me, but the shadows got her first. Darkness spread from my feet, seizing her in its grip. The door to the afterlife loomed behind me, closer than ever.

She gasped. "You can't kill me. You aren't allowed to take a soul to the afterlife if the person isn't dead."

"I'm not an official Reaper," I said. "The rules don't apply to me."

Hayley's composure cracked. "Help!"

As gratifying as it was to see her panic, I'd tormented her enough. I nodded to Allie, who conjured up a rope and bound Hayley's hands behind her back. "Is the detective on his way?"

"I told him to be here." Mart floated into view. "Give it two minutes."

At the sight of my brother, Hayley's panic turned to confusion. "What? You're not going to kill me?"

"That's your method, not mine," I said to her. "We already have your confession, but is there anything else you want to admit to before the police get here?"

"I don't understand why you did it," Carey said, looking at Hayley. "Why would you kill someone to get their powers? Weren't your own enough?"

"Her mother was dying," said Allie. "We all felt pity for her at the time, and while Mandy's death was tragic, I didn't think Hayley had it in her to commit murder. When I hired her, I never would have guessed she'd attempted to steal her powers. She had no gift for healing."

"The first ritual didn't work," I said. "Her power didn't transfer. She left the coven rather than risk being found out, and that was when the case was dropped. I think we got the rest. Right, Carey?"

She lifted her ghost goggles and gave a nod. Her camera had recorded the whole thing.

Hayley's eyes bulged. "What—?"

A growl sounded, then several werewolves ran into the room, circling Hayley. Drew walked in behind them, in human form.

"Carey just recorded Hayley's confession on her camera," I said. "Want to hear it?"

"Does that count as evidence?" asked Allie.

"Yes," he said. "Bring it with you to the police station, Carey."

Two of the shifters herded Hayley out of the room between them, while Drew turned to me. "Are you okay?"

"Sure," I said. "I'll be there in five, okay? I just need to deal with one small thing first."

"The ghost?" Carey guessed.

Drew gave a nod of understanding. "I'll see you later."

While Carey and her mother left with the police, I

headed in the opposite direction, across the bridge and towards the Reaper's home.

Old Harold was exactly where I'd left him, standing outside his cottage with an expectant look on his face and Mandy's ghost hovering behind him.

"Dealt with your little problem?" he asked.

I nodded. "Yeah. Mandy, I found your killer. She's on her way to jail now."

Mandy's expression crumpled, and silent tears flowed down her cheeks. "Thank you. Are… are you going to banish me now?"

"Not if you'd rather stay," I said. "But I can take you to see your sister first, if you like."

Mandy's ghost floated up to me. "Are you sure?"

"Of course I'm sure." I smiled at her. "I'll take you to see her."

There was no danger of us being followed, not with Hayley already in custody. My brother's ghost accompanied us, though he didn't have to, while I met Drew on the way to Mandy's sister's house. She answered the door after the third knock, wearing a dressing gown.

Her mouth parted when she set eyes on me. "I… did you find her?"

"We found your sister's killer," I told her. "She's on her way to jail right now. I also have your sister's ghost behind me, and she'd like to speak to you before she moves on."

Her eyes brimmed over. "How? I can't see her."

"I can help." I dropped my voice. "I'm a Reaper. Half of one, anyway. I can make you able to see her, if you like."

She nodded, and I let the shadows creep from my feet

until they surrounded her doorstep. Mandy floated closer and closer to me until the shadows enfolded her, too.

Her sister gasped. "I see her."

"Good." I stepped back. "You two can have as long to say goodbye as you need. I'll be right here."

And so would the door to the next world, when Mandy was ready.

The detective's hand found my shoulder as I watched the siblings approach one another, tears stinging my eyes. "I didn't know you could do this."

"It's not usual," I said. "Actually, it's kind of against half the Reapers' rulebook, but it's not like they're going to check up on me."

"I thought not." A chuckle entered his voice. "You don't do things by halves, do you? Reaper or witch."

"No, I really don't." I smiled at the sisters as they said their goodbyes, heedless of the shadows around them.

Maybe my Reaper talents weren't all bad.

16

"What do you mean, she's gone?" I said in disbelief. "Mina Devlin did a runner? Seriously?"

"She must have left the town the moment it became clear she wouldn't be able to keep this quiet," said Allie. "Hayley's actions against us were the last straw."

The two of us sat at the table in the restaurant, with Carey and her familiar. It'd been a hectic few days, and I'd been on tenterhooks waiting to hear of Mina resurfacing to make trouble for me. I hadn't realised she'd be cowardly enough to abandon what was left of her coven and run for the hills before any of the consequences found their way back to her.

"I thought Hayley was lying or exaggerating." I groaned. "Seriously? Mina gets away with covering up three murders and whatever else she did to secure her position as coven leader?"

"I wouldn't say she got away with it," said Allie. "Her coven is in tatters, and she won't be able to take on a position of authority within any other magical community. They'd ask for her history, which would lead them straight back here."

"One piece of good news, then," I said.

"The other is that we all got out alive," said Carey.

"You did great with the camera, though," I told her. "And Casper was amazing. Going after a murderer was much braver than going after a ghost."

Casper mewed and huddled closer to her. The two had been inseparable since the incident, including during their report to the police. While we had Hayley's confession on tape, the police

had still needed to hear a statement from the witnesses, including me.

"The weird thing is the story actually got me more readers," she said. "I thought admitting there wasn't a ghost in the house would end up with everyone abandoning my blog in droves, but they really got into the story about us unearthing a years-old murder."

"You did mention the ghost, though," I reminded her. "Even if we didn't get any footage of her."

After deliberation, we'd shared a version of the story of Healey House's history on her blog, with enough details omitted to remove anything which might cause her readers to figure out who'd been involved in the cover-up. Even with Mina gone from town, she was still dangerous enough to make trouble for us.

"True," she said. "I guess the part about us being trapped in a creepy old house was enough to satisfy the ghost fanatics."

"Pity we didn't get more footage of the ghost when she

was in my room," I said. "Glad she's gone, though, just for Mart's sake."

After she'd departed, he'd decided to take her room for his own, which was good news for both of us.

"We'll need someone new to take her place at the restaurant," said Allie. "Assuming anyone wants to work with us after we hired a murderer."

"Nobody will think bad of you for this," I reassured her. "You couldn't have known. Besides, everything's a bit unsettled at the moment."

With the coven minus a leader, the local witch and wizard population had some adjusting to do. I didn't know if they'd reform a new coven in place of the old one, or if they were too afraid of Mina's wrath to do so in case she came back and hexed all of them. The police were still on the lookout for her, but she was a formidable witch and no doubt had places to hide. On the plus side, the restaurant's business hadn't visibly suffered, and the local wizards continued to meet here.

"You aren't wrong," said Allie. "I think a certain group of former coven members might need a side income if this shakes out the way I think it might."

"Like them?" Carey indicated the group of wizards who'd just entered. Among them was Archie, who caught my eye.

I stepped away from the others as the wizard approached me. "I just wanted to say thank you," he said to me. "For getting answers on Harriet's death."

"No worries," I said.

"Also, thanks for chasing that evil Mina Devlin out of town," added Bernard. "None of us will miss her."

"That part wasn't exactly deliberate," I admitted, "but

at least she can't stop you from forming your own coven now."

Anyone would be able to do the same. Granted, it was bound to cause issues between me and the other ex-coven members. Cathy in particular had suffered a grilling at the police's hands for her involvement in the cover-up, though I hadn't heard an update from the detective yet. I'd better hope I didn't need a doctor in future, in case she tried to poison me.

Carey cleared her throat and indicated the doors. I looked that way and already knew who I'd see waving back. *Speak of the devil and he shall appear.*

Ignoring Mart's wolf-whistle from behind me, I joined the detective outside.

"How was the trial?" I asked him.

"Hayley is in jail," he said. "Cathy is going to have a short sentence, too, for her involvement in the cover-up. She showed genuine remorse, but working closely with the coven leader has consequences."

"For everyone but Mina, apparently," I said.

"My team has been searching the area," he said.

"I know, but werewolves can only go so far on foot," I said. "She probably flew away. Or used magic to teleport."

"Even in the magical world, she can't hide forever," he said. "We'll get her. Mark my words."

"I hope so," I said. "She's sneaky, that's for sure. And now Allie needs new bar staff, which I suppose will give the other coven members something to do. If they don't blame us for the loss of their leader, anyway."

"I notice you didn't mention any of that in the official story," he said. "Good thinking."

"How do you know…?" I broke off. "You're still reading Carey's blog, aren't you?"

He shot me a smile. "I feel it's nice to be supportive. Besides, I was interested to see which bit you wrote."

"We both wrote it," I told him. "We had to leave out the details of the coven members, including the victims. I kept it all vague, but even then, it's a popular story."

"Did you help Mandy's ghost, then?" he asked.

"Yeah, I helped her move on. After she said goodbye to her sister, anyway."

We walked past the cemetery. Harriet had been buried, and Mandy's family now had closure. As for the Reaper? He'd let me get on with my job without a fuss, for a wonder.

"He looked after her," I remarked to Drew, with a glance at his cottage. "Mandy, I mean. He told me he didn't want to get involved in coven drama, but he still made sure nobody banished her."

"I have an inkling our Reaper cares more for the spirits than he lets on."

He probably wasn't wrong. Old Harold and I weren't friends, not even close, but we'd managed to cooperate for once, and maybe he'd be less unfriendly in future. I could dream.

Speaking of dreams… it was about time I got things straight with the detective.

I drew in a breath. "Well, now the case is over, you're out of excuses to spend time around me."

"I wouldn't say that," he said. "I'd like to take you out tonight."

My heart missed a beat. "Really?"

"What do you think?" said Drew. "Want to give it a shot?"

I returned his smile and thought *why not.* I'd give it a shot. I was here in Hawkwood Hollow for the long haul, I knew that, now. It was time to take a leap of faith.

I slipped my hand into his, and we turned our back the Reaper's cottage and walked away.

ABOUT THE AUTHOR

Elle Adams lives in the middle of England, where she spends most of her time reading an ever-growing mountain of books, planning her next adventure, or writing. Elle's books are humorous mysteries with a paranormal twist, packed with magical mayhem.

She also writes urban and contemporary fantasy novels as Emma L. Adams.

Find Elle on Facebook at https://www.facebook.com/pg/ElleAdamsAuthor/

Or sign up to her newsletter at: smarturl.it/ElleAdamsNewsletter

Printed in Great Britain
by Amazon